Love's Following

Sea

The Pyefleet Chronicles: 10

CLIVE HAZELL

authorHOUSE®

AuthorHouse™
1663 Liberty Drive
Bloomington, IN 47403
www.authorhouse.com
Phone: 1 (800) 839-8640

Published by AuthorHouse 04/24/2019

ISBN: 978-1-7283-0901-9 (sc)
ISBN: 978-1-7283-0900-2 (e)

Library of Congress Control Number: 2019904672

Print information available on the last page.

Chapter 1

I

The rain clouds seemed to come from out of nowhere. Rose had started off when the sun was shining brightly to take the cardigan she had just knitted for Parson Highweather. No sooner had she dropped it off to Kitty, the Parson's daughter, than the skies clouded over.

"I had better be off, before the rain sets in. Lady Charlotte will be missing me by now for certain."

Kitty was disappointed, for they were like sisters. Her parents had all but adopted her when her mother took ill and died and father turned to gin, winding up in the back alleys of London, or who knows where.

The long, curving sea wall lay before her. The sea on the left was grey and troubled and beyond the spinney of poplars and the salt marsh where hundreds of widgeon were turning into the freshly risen wind, she could see the shroud of grey rain approaching. She hastened, feeling the wind get colder and starting to slap her cotton frock about her.

As if drawn by a cord the curtain of rain swept over her and soon she was soaked through, the dress clinging to her. Cold and shivering, she pushed open the old iron gate, rusting on its hinges, and started to run up the lane to the hall. Just as she was turning off to the servant's quarters where she knew the innumerable labours of the scullery maid awaited her, she heard, with a dull sinking feeling in her stomach, the call she had come to dread.

"Rose! Come here! I need you, this minute!"

She stopped dead in her tracks and, ensuring that none of her true feelings would show on her face, she turned. It was Sir Sydney, standing in the shelter of the porticos of the old manor. He gestured to her to come towards him.

"Come here my girl, a word, if you please."

She approached, and, as she did, she saw the old familiar leer in his eye. He feigned friendliness with his grin, but it could not conceal his darker feelings—his contempt, his hunger and, underneath it all, his desperation and loneliness.

"My, my, how you have grown! Truly blossoming! How old are you now?"

He had repeated these comments some hundred times but Rose dutifully replied.

"Twenty, sir." She became painfully aware that she was soaking wet and cold. Her frock was clinging to her body. His eyes wandered freely, greedily and with impunity, over her. She shivered and it seemed to her that he enjoyed her shiver, taking it perhaps for a shiver of fright as much as a shiver of cold.

There was a prolonged silence as it seemed that he had run out of words. "As if his brain has turned off", bethought Rose. She endured his gaze. Her hair streamed over her face. She wondered if this would never end. Surely soon he would get embarrassed.

But no. He continued. "Let me see," he mused aloud. "You must be about five foot three and weigh about eight stone now?"

Rose felt her soul shrinking into the tiniest most secretive part of herself. "I am sure I do not know, sir", she muttered.

"As fine a girl as we have here at Pyefleet, I'll warrant! Let me see your eyes. All the work has made you sturdy too. Look at me, girl."

Rose felt her eyes start to brim with tears, against her will, for she did not wish to show the man he had any power over her. She clenched her jaw to stop its trembling and looked up.

"Ah! Yes, perfection—what is it they say? Robin's egg blue and, my word! Your hair is the same brown as the splotches on a robin's egg. But wait. Do I see defiance? Well my lass, we will have to do something about that I…"

"Sir! What are you doing? Get in here immediately. Squire Paxton is waiting for you."

It was Lady Charlotte. She must have witnessed his leering, lurid gaze. Rose's heart sank again. Once again Lady Charlotte would have it in for her, asking her to do all kinds of impossible menial tasks, as if to get revenge since she seemed certain that it was Rose who had instigated the entire exchange, preying upon her husband's weakness. Lady Charlotte had never forgiven her husband for many wrongdoings. The latest one was his inveighing against the parson, threatening with the loss of his job if he did not let "orphan Rose" come and work at the manor. Parson Highweather felt he had no choice since he had responsibilities and dependents at the workhouse. He complied with Sir Sydney while vowing to keep a close watch on Rose's well-being.

Sir Sydney cleared his throat, shrugged his shoulders, recomposed himself and left. Rose ran through the still pouring rain back to the servants' quarters.

"My Lord!" exclaimed Mrs. Moffett, the cook. "You are soaked through. Let me help dry you before you catch your death of cold."

When Rose had changed into dry clothes she helped Mrs. Moffett prepare the dinner of rabbit stew and turnips. Slowly the steamy heat of the kitchen eased into Rose's bones. She realized the cold had come not only from the sudden rain but also from the chill of Sir Sydney and Lady Charlotte. She became aware that this cold empty feeling had been part of life from the time she had lost her mother. Certainly the love of those around her, right now Mrs. Moffett with her warm and bustling ways, earlier Kitty and the Parson's family, with their kindness and concern and, of course, her Garrad, the very thought of whom filled her emptiness. All this, however could be so easily swept aside by an encounter of coldness of usage such as the one she had just had on the steps with "Lord and Lady Muck" as Mrs. Moffett referred to them under her breath, in private.

II

The rain had gusted away overnight and the whole landscape shone. Far over the fields Rose could see the flocks of dunlin weave and then suddenly flash over the waters of the estuary. She was carrying the vegetable peelings to the pigs beyond the stable.

As she passed the stable, she saw her Garrad, the groom. He was methodically, carefully sweeping the curry-comb over the glistening flanks of Lady Charlotte's chestnut mare. Rose found herself admiring his broad shoulders, flexing as the curry-comb swept across the horse's flanks, bringing forth a glistering shine. Suddenly, the horse started, perhaps sensing that Rose was approaching.

"Careful there, Mr. Hansen," she called out to Garrad. "For she is a spirited lady!"

"Like someone else I know," he replied.

Rose smiled knowingly. "Oh. And just who might that be?" she inquired.

"In truth, I cannot say, save that I respect and admire her greatly."

Rose smiled. This was their secret way of saying, and yet not saying, how smitten they were with each other.

At this very point, Lady Charlotte came out from behind the stable. Perhaps she had been there all along. Rose's heart sank once again for it was rumored that Lady Charlotte had a soft spot for groom Garrad Hansen. It was understandable. He was strong, good humored, honest and the best groom in the parish. Many a heart fluttered when he was nearby.

"Garrad, is my horse ready?" she asked sharply, without so much as a glance in Rose's direction.

"She is, my lady. And she is well-rested. Be careful along the sea wall and the crags, for the night-rain may have washed them out. Also they are building out by the Martello tower."

"Thank you, Garrad. One day we shall have to ride together, you and I. You may show me all your secret spots."

Garrad blushed and Rose's eyes narrowed despite her best attempts to hide her feelings.

Lady Charlotte mounted the horse, drove in the spurs and trotted off.

"Oh, do be careful my lady." mimicked Rose, poking fun at Garrad's subservience. "Watch out for Bonaparte at the Martello tower!"

All along the coast, towers and emplacements were being built as a protection from the feared invasion of Napoleon Bonaparte. Children were told to be good or "Old Boney will come and get you in the night." Aristocrats and royalty were all in fear of an invasion or even an uprising as the fever of revolution spread across the continent.

Garrad shrugged and smiled. He was used to Rose's spirited ways. He loved them as he loved the spirit in his horses.

"You should be off attending to your pigs." He jibed.

"You mean my other pigs," she clipped back at him and she turned on her heels and set off briskly for the sty. Garrad laughed deeply, feeling a truly lucky man.

III

Rose had two hours off from her duties as scullery maid. Mrs. Moffett had told her to be off and go for a walk, to clear out the cobwebs. Accordingly, Rose went to the shoreline, to the cliffs of the Red Crag.

The tide was out and Avocets, Curlew, Whimbrel and Oystercatchers were poking at the waterline, far across the mud flats. Nearer, Dunlin nervously pecked at the tide-wrack. She loved the Crag. It was a young sandstone.

Crumbly as an oatmeal biscuit, it was loaded with fossils from its days as a beach millions of years ago, or at least so she had been told by Parson Highweather one Sunday when he lead a group of parishioners and delivered a guided tour of these strange orange cliffs that seemed so out of place abutting, as they did, the expansive flatness of the Essex marshes. She had only gone on that field trip with the Parson so that she could be with Garrad, who insisted on going to hear the latest on the new science of geology.

She wove her way up the cobbles and gravel of the beach toward the orange-red crag where she curiously poked at the shells that protruded from its eroding face. They were blanched white and almost the consistency of chalk. She thought of starting a collection, like the scientists do.

Out of the corner of her eye she saw a movement, a shadow. It was Garrad.

"I thought you would be down here," he said with his gently rolling, sing-song Essex accent.

"Get a breath of fresh salt air, good for the spirit," she replied, still busying herself with what looked like a blanched oyster-shell protruding from the cliff-face.

"Ah yes," he assented. He took a deep breath and took in the whole scene—the huge sky, the rust-colored sails of the barges out on the fleet, the wading birds, the trickle of the tide as it shifted. Then, with a start, as if an idea had just come to him, he said, "Just whistle and I'll come running!"

"I beg your pardon?" inquired Rose.

"Just whistle and I'll come running! The old story of these cliffs."

All Rose could do was give him a puzzled, impatient look.

"The old story. There was this old chap came down to these cliffs and, just like you, he started poking around. All of a sudden, he comes upon a whistle, made out of clay it was. He carefully digs it out and rubs it clean. What does he see on it but some writing? It said 'Just whistle and I'll come running.' Of course, he thinks nothing of it. So shakes the whistle free of sand and gives it a puff. Sure enough it works— a strange high pitched sound—almost like a dog whistle. He puts the whistle in his pocket and sets off home. As he is walking down the beach he gets a funny feeling. He looks behind him and sees something or someone in the far distance, following him down the strand. He goes home and he still feels that strange presence in his house. He starts to think he is going mad. Chairs are moved around. Windows he left open are closed. His tools are packed away when he knows that he left them out. Even when he goes down the pub, he feels this presence, even as if someone nudges him. Try as he might he cannot be rid of this presence in his life. And of course, everybody thinks he is mad."

"Where did you hear this story?" asked Rose.

"I cannot say as how I remember. I've known it since I was a child. But it certainly gives you the creeps about this place. Imagine how horrible that would be. To be pursued like that, relentlessly," and Garrad gave an involuntary shiver.

"To me, it sounds like true love. When he blew the whistle, he called forth love in that spirit who then just followed him forever, to the ends of the earth, for all time."

"Hmm," said Garrad. "I never looked at it in that light. Hmm! So you believe in true love?"

"Perhaps," replied Rose and in a rare shy moment, she blushed and looked at the crag.

Finally, she looked up only to meet Garrad's gaze which was laden with tenderness and meaning. "I should like to kiss you," he said softly.

"All right then," she replied and closed her eyes and offered her lips.

And they kissed, gently at first, like fluttering birds and then more intensely, deeply and passionately. Garrad smelled of leather and the stables and she of soap and the scullery. These smells seemed to mingle as their bodies became one. Rose felt her legs give way and, at this, broke away, straightening her dress and bodice.

"I must be back," she whispered, almost to herself.

"Of course. But there is something I must tell you…"

"I know what it is, and I feel the same. One day soon, we will be free of this and have our own few acres, I can feel it."

Rose finally extricated the bleached ancient oyster shell. She dusted it off, put it in her pocket and started for the house. Garrad, still thinking, followed.

"Well my lovely, just whistle and I'll come running," said Garrad, smiling as they hastened down the strand towards the style that opened up on to the pathway to the house.

IV

Rose finally finished ironing and folding the linens for the house. The sun had long since set, but it was hot in the scullery. She raised her forearm to mop her brow. Mrs.

Moffett bustled in and said, "All done, my dear? No rest for the wicked?"

"I know," replied Rose. "I'll sleep tonight."

"I think I saw Garrad out by the greenhouses," said Mrs. Moffett, knowingly.

"Ah! Maybe I shall get a breath of fresh air," said Rose, smiling.

"You do, my dear, I shall finish up here."

Rose took off her pinafore and stepped out into the evening air. She breathed in deeply. The breeze wafted in the smells from the sea and marshes across the fields and water-meadows. The sharp tang of the tide wrack enlivened her.

Garrad was standing by the greenhouses, leaning against a fencepost, gazing up at the stars which seemed to be peeking out from behind the purple clouds that were heading east, out over the North Sea.

"Dreaming?" asked Rose.

"Oh! Hello. No, just wondering if they see the same stars everywhere."

"Thinking of travelling, are we?" said Rose, cheeky as usual.

"Oh no, my future is here. I am an Essex boy," and he smiled at her.

"Let us go and watch the moon rise over the barrow."

"In an adventuresome mood are we? Maybe we'll see the sword-dancing Viking ghost?"

"Maybe," replied Rose. "But I just need to be away from this place. It oppresses me so."

They followed the sea wall up the channel which tinkled like a thousand small bells as the tide changed and soon found themselves at the barrow, an ancient burial mound, topped with a thicket of pines, a round hummock rising above the surrounding marshy flats. The climb up the barrow-side was quite steep and by the time they had reached its curved top they were puffing.

They sat on a fallen log amongst the pines. In the distance, across the channel, they could see the first rays of the rising moon as it rose above the fretted grey-brown clouds. As they caught their breath, they composed themselves and took in the scene. A moon track was starting to show, twinkling across the inky waters. Coots were croaking and the occasional peewit gave a plaintive cry.

"It's quite beautiful isn't it?" said Garrad quietly, so as not to disturb the mood.

"Yes," replied Rose, "But I wish I could take it all in like you."

"How do you mean?"

"I feel like sometimes I am separated from the world as if by a glass pane."

"I think I know that feeling. I have had it sometimes when I am very sad."

"Yes. Perhaps that is it. What was that word you told me the other day? The French word—for the hole they put you in?"

"Oubliette."

"Yes. I sometimes feel as though I have been in an oubliette all my life. I am here on the surface, but somehow not here, like the deepest part of me has been left behind forgotten. Maybe…"

"I know, maybe you felt forgotten by your parents. Even though they did not forget you. They were taken away, but as a child you may have thought that."

11

"That makes sense to me. Except for when I am with you, my love. When you are near, or when you touch me, it's like I come to life again and that deep hidden forgotten part of me comes back to the surface and I can take all of this in."

"Thank you my love. I am honored to be the one who has the key to your oubliette."

Rose smiled and took a deep breath. As she exhaled she seemed to let go of a deep tension in her body and she relaxed. A small boat was bobbing across the channel, its light jogging up and down as if dancing a hornpipe. Rose smiled.

"What was that other word you learned? The one about the imp in the darkness? The little chap who guides us in the void?"

"Telesphorus. Tonight I am quite the dictionary," replied Garrad.

Rose started to tear up as the thought crystallized for her. "You are my telesphorus, Garrad. I should be lost, cast adrift without you."

"I shall try to keep shining in the blackness for you, no matter what, my precious." And he reached out his hand. They held hands quietly for some time.

"Your hands are so soft," she finally said. "Mine are so cracked and sore from all the scullery work. Quite soon I shall have housemaid's knees and elbows."

"Oh I think we shall be done with this soon enough," replied Garrad. "I know. I think my hands are soft from rubbing all the dubbin into the saddles and bridles. Look. The moon is up now. Any sign of our dancing Viking warrior?"

"Not yet. Why do you think he stays here?"

"I do not know. Perhaps his ghost stays here because he is still fighting a battle of, what, a thousand years ago? Or perhaps his lady-love is buried beneath us and he is dancing for her."

"It gives me the willies."

"No fear, my pigeon. Anyway, I think we are expected back at the house by now."

They clambered cautiously down the steep slope of the barrow and headed back along the sea wall. The waters and birds were still now, as they crossed the stile and made their way down the side of the greenhouse.

A sudden footfall and a voice raised stopped them in their tracks. A look at each other quickly told them to be quiet, for if it was Sir Sydney or Lady Charlotte, it would almost certainly mean trouble for them.

The voices grew louder and they settled on the other side of the greenhouse. It was indeed Sir Sydney, and Lady Charlotte, but there were also two other voices. Trying to make out the conversation and also attempting to see how they might extricate themselves from this situation undetected, they froze. One voice was that of Squire Paxton, a neighbor and associate of Sir Sydney's. The fourth voice they could not identify.

The conversation, as far as they could tell, was something about the towers. Some of the words they could not make out, like "noovo" and "toor". It was as if they were changing the language they were speaking in mid-sentence. What the language was they did not know, nor could they make out completely what it was they were speaking of. They just knew for certain that they must get out of there quickly and quietly. The conversants started to raise their voices, as if a quarrel was breaking out. Over what, Rose and Garrad had no idea. They looked at each other and almost giggled at the silliness of their situation. They took advantage of the raised voices to start to creep away. At one point the speakers stopped and the third member, the stranger said something like, "Key eh la? Key eh la?" repeating this several times. Rose and Garrad froze, waited and eventually the conversation recommenced.

Minutes later, they were at the scullery door. Relieved and with quite enough adventure for one day, they exchanged tender glances that spoke volumes of their feelings for each other and parted.

V

Garrad was up early the next morning. Something had startled the horses so he rose to see to them. He did not mind for he had to prepare Sir Sydney's horse. Once he had calmed the horses, he stepped outside to savour the crisp morning air which so sharply contrasted with the damp, thick heat of the stable. As he gazed out across the water-meadows and beyond across the Pyefleet Channel an unfamiliar boat caught his eye. The Essex marshes were renowned for the smuggling that took place there. Long mud-banked channels wound their way deep inland. Smugglers who knew their way could row up these to various public houses and cottages where they could hide their contraband. There were stories of old farm ponds that had been dug deep so the smugglers could sink their wares in bottles wrapped up in sacks at the end of a rope to avoid the revenue men.

But this boat was different, perhaps something to do with the voices last night…Garrad shrugged his shoulders and turned to the stable and started work on the horses.

An hour later, Sir Sydney came down from the house and Garrad lead the steed out to him. Lady Charlotte stood at the doorway to bid him farewell.

"Far to ride today, my lord?" inquired Garrad.

"Just to Maldon, I have business there."

"Very good, sir." Garrad stroked the horse's glossy, light-brown neck. "You'll find Boudicca here to be in fine fettle and up to the task."

But Boudicca seemed restive. As Sir Sydney approached, she snorted and kicked. Garrad tried to calm her but each time Sir Sydney took a step towards her she became even more agitated.

"My, my!" said Garrad, trying to ease the mounting tension. "She is living up to her name today." Boudicca was the warlike queen of the Iceni tribe who had rebelled and sacked nearby Roman Colchester.

"Thank you for your amusing comments. Perhaps if you had spent more time with her and less on your history books, she would be better behaved," retorted Sir Sydney. "What she needs is some discipline! A damn good thrashing would teach her some manners!"

"Oh, begging your pardon, Sir, I think not, I think she is just afeared of something," said Garrad consolingly, praying that the ever more boisterous Boudicca would calm down.

Sir Sydney became even more irate and angrily snatched the bridle from Garrad's hand. "I'll teach you obedience, missy!" he said through gritted teeth, and he wrenched the bridle so hard the bit cut Boudicca's lips. At this Boudicca reared up. Both Garrad and Sir Sydney stepped back but Sir Sydney's face was scratched by a hoof. He fell to the ground while Garrad stepped close to Boudicca and calmed the snorting horse whose eyes were wide and tilted in fear. Sir Sydney retreated and Garrad calmed Boudicca down.

"I think I should get you another horse, sir. Perhaps Matilda. She is ready." Said Garrad as he led Boudicca back into the stable.

"Yes." groaned Sir Sydney, nursing his face and shoulder, and retreating to the house.

Lady Charlotte, who had been witnessing all this from the steps at the end of the gravel pathway leading up to the great house, stepped back, smirking as he came up the steps of the house.

"I shall have that horse shot!" said Sir Sydney, bitterly.

"You shall do no such thing!" retorted Lady Charlotte. "She is my prize. And if you were any kind of man like Garrad Hansen, you would be able to understand and manage her." She secretly took great pleasure in this last remark, not realizing that at its utterance, she had done great harm to Garrad, whom she desired. For at that instant Sir Sydney's chronic grudging resentment of Garrad blossomed into a full-blown hatred and a determination to destroy him. He turned and glared at both Garrad and Boudicca. He caught Lady Charlotte smiling with what seemed like a look of victory and stormed into the house.

VI

On Sunday afternoon, Garrad and Rose had two hours of free time. It was blustery but they decided to walk along the sea wall to visit Parson Highweather.

"So what are your exact plans, Garrad Hansen," asked Rose with a mock challenge.

"Well," he replied, "I shall work here for a while longer, then, when I have enough saved, I intend to buy some land and farm it."

"On your own?" she pressed.

"Oh, I don't know," he teased. "Perhaps I shall marry and have children. I might need the help." He could barely restrain a smile as he said this.

"Well, I hope you find someone suitable," retorted Rose, meeting his challenge. "I am sure there is some unsuspecting miss who will be fooled into taking you."

Garrad laughed at this, as they turned up the pathway to the Parson's.

Parson Highweather greeted them heartily. "Come in, come in young people!" he exclaimed. "I have something to show you." And he led them into his study. "Look at these!" and he gestured towards an array of fossils. "I have been reading the work of Hutton on geology and have decided to follow this as my avocation…"

But he was interrupted by his wife who bustled in. "Oh my! Please spare these young folks your lectures! Let us retire to the parlour and have some tea. You, sir, must rest anyway before your sermon this evening."

"Quite, my dear," smiled the Parson. And they proceeded to the parlour which was well lit, having an enormous window overlooking the channel. Garrad paused gazing afar at the barges and fishing boats still plying on the full tide.

Just as they sat down and as Mrs. Highweather was pouring the tea, their daughter Kitty came in. Rose jumped up and hugged her, saying, "Sister! How are you? My, how your brow is furrowed."

"French," replied Kitty. "I have been learning, of all things, French."

"They may be our adversaries, but it is a beautiful language with many wise exponents, Lafontaine, for example, who said, 'When nature is pushed out the window, it will force its way back through the door..'" said Parson Highweather, firmly.

"Thank you my dear, edifying, as always," interrupted Mrs. Highweather, smiling wryly.

"My! French, so courtly! Do treat us to a word or two," said Rose.

And Kitty spoke. "Comment vous-appelez-vous. Enchanté. Au revoir."

Both Garrad and Rose started. "Goodness," said Rose. "That is just like what we heard the other night, isn't it Garrad?" Garrad nodded.

"Where?" asked Parson Highweather.

"Out by the greenhouse. Sir Sydney, Squire Paxton and milady were talking to some man, and it sounded just like that. They didn't notice us. We didn't want to be discovered. It was strange wasn't it Garrad?" Garrad nodded.

"Really? And when was this?" asked the Parson. His interest was clearly piqued.

"Thursday night," said Garrad. "Why?"

"Oh, nothing. I am sure it is of no consequence," replied the Parson but there was a silence. Something was on his mind.

Mrs. Highweather broke the silence. "So what biscuit would you like, Garrad? Ginger snap or oatmeal?"

"Time for a song!" announced Parson Highweather. "Rose, do play for us! It has been so long."

"Yes, do," pleaded Kitty in mock seriousness, "It will smooth my furrowed brow."

"Alright," said Rose and she put down her teacup and walked over to the upright piano the Parson used to practice hymns and at which she had played for hours as a girl. Garrad felt his chin melt and his heart swell. He loved her playing and singing so much, it almost moved him to tears.

Rose started to play, "Lowlands Away." It was a strange mournful song, in a minor key, a song about lost love and terrible dreams that one's beloved had died in a distant land. It seemed an odd choice for such a bright day and such jolly company but somehow all felt it was appropriate as it perhaps emanated from deep within Rose, whose mother had died so young and whose father had become quite bereft of his senses and abandoned her. None spoke of this to Rose, but all recognized it, especially the wife of Parson Highweather who had insisted on taking in young Rose at the age of three and raising her as if she were their very own. The song, sad and strange as it was, thus became a living indicator of Rose's deep sadness and how she had mastered it to become the beautiful young woman she was.

The last chord, an E minor, rang out through the parsonage for what seemed to be an eternity, fading so slowly into a near silence broken only by the distant croak of a pheasant out in the fields. Finally Mrs. Scofield, like a froth of lace and linen, bustled in bearing a broad silver tray.

"Crumpets, for those as is interested," she announced as she placed the tray on the end table. "Shall I top up the hot water for the tea, Mum?"

"Thank you Mrs. Scofield. Yes. That would be wonderful," replied Mrs. Highweather.

Again, there was silence as attention was placed on the crumpets, butter and home-made jams and the only noise was of cutlery and crockery and careful, decorous eating.

An hour or so later, when the low sun seemed to be rolling along the mudbanks of the channel, Rose said that she and Garrad must get back to the manor.

"So terrible, Rose," tutted Mrs. Highweather. "Why do you have to go? You know you have a place with us. John," she addressed her husband, the parson, "Why does she have to go? They are so…so…" She could not complete the sentence. Her Christian virtue prevented her from casting aspersions.

"Now, now my dear. We have visited this before. Of course she is welcome here at all times and to stay for all her life, but, as you know, Sir Sydney would have her working over there and Sir Sydney wields considerable influence, why my very position…"

"Scoundrels, all of them," Mrs. Highweather was finally able to exclaim. "If they do not stop their ways, we shall soon be as it is in France. May the good Lord help us!"

"Now, now, my dear. No careless talk. Let us finish this wonderful afternoon on an inspiring note," implored Parson Highweather.

Mrs. Highweather agreed, but not without some rearranging of her skirts and her lace handkerchief. Rose finally broke the spell and stood up with Garrad.

"We must be going. Thank you so much, for a delightful afternoon."

At this the ladies hugged and the men shook hands. The parson, his wife and Kitty gazed at Garrad and Rose as they walked down the path and out on to the sea wall, happy to see the loving couple together and yet sad and concerned at their placement at Pyefleet Manor.

VII

A brisk North-Easterly wind ruffled the grey waters of the Pyefleet channel as Squire Paxton, dismounted his horse. He had spurred it needlessly and Garrad noticed the bleeding flanks as he led the unfortunate beast away.

It was as if the Squire knew that he was being silently rebuked by Garrad, for he looked at him contemptuously as he took off his riding gloves.

"Hail, Paxton!" called out Sir Sydney from the steps of the house.

"Hail," responded Paxton, flatly.

Sydney had seen the way Paxton looked at Garrad and said, "I know. He's a rum fellow, if you ask me. Comes from reading too much. Of course all the women adore him. I can't stand the chap. I'd like to see him transported."

"Australia, eh? Yes, that's the ticket, old chap. Get rid of him. These types are trouble-makers—reform and all that. They won't do us the kind service of going to America or somewhere on their own so we have to send them to

Australia, van Deimen's land or somewhere. The old ways are dying and we're under siege. Must be nipped in the bud."

"Hah! Well said, old man. Let's go inside. I have a very good sherry waiting. You can tell me all about your conquests in London"

They both laughed and Paxton stepped inside the house. Sir Sydney paused on the steps, gazing across the grey, flecked waters of the channel. He nodded to himself in quiet resolve.

VIII

The following week Sir Sydney donned his hunting attire and trudged out to the blinds at Fingrinhoe Spinney. He shot four pheasants. When he came home he gave two of them to Mrs. Moffet and asked her to prepare them for that evening's meal.

When night fell he slipped out and placed the other two dead birds in Garrad Hansen's haversack in the barn. The next morning, under the pretext of inspecting his horses, he went to the barn with Frederick, the stable-boy, and found the pheasants in Garrad's haversack. He accused Garrad of poaching, specifically poaching on Squire Paxton's land. He claimed to have heard on good authority that he had been seen in the vicinity.

Constable Pike was summoned and Garrad was taken off. Paxton was summoned to the station and backed up Sir Sydney's story. Rose had been out on the mudflats gathering cockles at low tide while all this was going on.

Mrs. Moffett sent the stable-boy out to fetch her and broke the news to her on her return. Rose fainted on the spot, as if the very soul had been driven out of her. Mrs. Moffett and Travis, the butler, carried her to her room where she lay, semi-conscious, sobbing deliriously until evening fell, when, mercifully, she fell asleep.

IX

Mrs. Moffett woke Rose the next morning.

"Here, my dove, I made your tea. Hot and sweet. You must be up and about your business. I know it must be hard, but you and I know it will all come out right in the end."

Rose stirred and turned, her hair in disarray. "How can you be so sure? I am starting to think they are all against him. I must go and see him. Where are they holding him?"

"I should imagine they have him bound over in Colchester by now. Ten miles away, and you know they won't let you go."

"I have such a bad premonition, Mrs. Moffett. I think they are going to destroy my Garrad."

"Oh, my dove, no. How could that be so? The two of you are so good…"

At this Frederick, the stable boy, came in downstairs and called up, "Sir Sydney's mother would see you, Rose."

Sir Sydney's mother, Catherine, the dowager marquess, had been bedridden for years now. Rose had been her steadfast companion. It was to the point where the lady considered Rose her closest relative for Rose was the one who would spend the longest time with her, reading to her on long dreary afternoons. She was in the words of her ladyship, "My one ray of sunshine. My linnet."

Rose pulled herself together and made her way across the gravel driveway to the big house, where she ascended the stairs to the remote corner where her ladyship lay in bed.

"Ah! Rose, my dear. I have just heard through Travis of what has transpired. Dreadful! Of course, it cannot be true. We both know what blackguards my son and Paxton are. I will do my best to intercede with the constable on Garrad's behalf."

"Thank you m'am." Replied Rose, curtseying.

"Oh! We'll have none of that. You are my boon, my only companion in what, I fear, are my last days here on this benighted clod. Please sit down, and let us take our minds off this nonsense. Read. Read Donne to me…over there. Yes, read the one on page forty four."

Rose fetched the leather-bound volume, worn from so many readings, and leafed through to page forty four.

"This is a new one," she said. "I so loved the last one we read. What was it called now?"

"Ah yes," replied Lady Catherine, brightening. "It was called 'A Nocturne Upon Saint Lucy's Eve.' I thought you might like it."

"Yes. It was so sad, so dark—all about the shrinking of the soul, down to the very bedpost. Yet somehow, even though it expressed the deepest sadness I can imagine, it made me feel better, as though I am not alone. As though someone else had those selfsame feelings that will occasionally overcome me, and that even though it was long ago that these sentiments were penned, I feel less alone in the world, as if I have a companion in the darkness."

"Beautifully put, my dear," replied Lady Catherine. "Yes Mr. Donne is a good companion indeed as are all of his fellows. Let us see what he has to inform us of today."

Rose started to read:

"A Valediction: Forbidding Mourning
As virtuous men pass mildly away,
And whisper to their souls to go,
Whilst some of their sad friends do say…"

"Do not be sad when I go," interrupted Lady Catherine. "That reminds me." And she felt under the coverlet and retrieved a brown envelope which she handed to Rose.

"This is for you. I apologize for my unconventional delivery, but I do not trust my son and daughter-in law. If I left you anything in my will I am sure they would prevent it. So, here. It is money. Enough to give you and Garrad a good start."

Rose was flabbergasted. She struggled for breath as she opened the envelope and encountered the three thick bundles of banknotes. "But ma'am!…"

"No, I'll heed no remonstrance. It is yours. You are the closest to me. You gave without counting the cost. This is yours. Guard it well. Enjoy your life with Garrad." At this she suddenly turned pale and gestured with a weakened hand towards the decanter at the bedside. Rose quickly poured a draught of the medicine which Lady Catherine swallowed. She calmed down.

"I must rest, now my dear. We will return to Mr. Donne later. I will intercede with regard to Garrad. Be hopeful, my dear."

"Yes ma'am," replied Rose and she retired clutching the envelope to her bodice as she almost stumbled down the sweeping staircase.

X

"You should go," said Mrs. Moffett, up to her elbows in sudsy water, "I shall be able to cover for you. I'll have Frederick prepare the pony for you. No-one will notice. The master of the house is still sleeping off his booze-up from celebrating last night. What? I don't know."

Rose paused, her arms full of pots and pans and her face, normally soft, temporarily hardened, as if by some deep resolution. "You are right," she replied. "I will go as soon as the pony is ready." Frederick, sitting by the stove, needed no encouragement. He ran off to get the pony ready.

Rose made her way at first behind the shelter of the sea wall, just to be sure that her departure would not be noticed. Soon she was out on the causeway to the mainland and on her way over the gently rolling verdant hills towards Colchester, and the gaol.

Arriving at the station in the high street, which was bustling with the weekly market, she entered the police station. The constable knew her from church and let her go downstairs into the cells. Down below, the air was thick and acrid and several men were groaning in pain.

"He's down there, at the end," said the constable. "I shall wait here. Keep your distance from these miscreants, miss."

Garrad had heard her coming so he stood, waiting at the bars of his cell. His tawny hair was tousled and matted and his face was stubbled, unshaven.

"Garrad!" she gasped. The sound came from a place so deep inside her that she momentarily felt it was the voice of another. Garrad's face softened and his eyes moistened with tears. They gazed at one another and both felt their breathing and hearts still as they seemed to melt into one. No words were necessary.

"This will soon be over," he said, finally.

Rose simply nodded, trying to stem the rising tide of tears filling her throat. Then she said, "Lady Catherine will speak up for you and she has hired a lawyer to gather character references, so I am sure you are right."

"Yes," he replied, "and we will be back to our old ways—at the crag, bird watching, on the barrow—building our future."

"I know," she replied.

"You know," said Garrad, brightening somewhat, "I had a dream last night. I think it was a premonition of what is to come. I dreamed it was just you and I on some beautiful lush pastureland, by a river, completely untouched, unspoiled by the depredations of human hands and we were to farm this land together. The river was full of fish…someone was helping us…it was so clear."

"That sounds lovely," she replied. "We must hold on to that dream, no matter what. Touch my hand and all will be well," and she put her hand flat between in the space between the bars.

Wordlessly, Garrad placed his hand gently on hers and they both felt a surge of calm joy course through their bodies, to the deepest reaches of their souls, and with this, both felt secure that no matter what, all would be well.

"Alright. That will do. Time's up," barked the policeman. "Let's go, miss, else I shall be in trouble."

Garrad nodded as if in assent and to let Rose know that he was alright and they broke the contact of their hands. Feeling her entire body contract, Rose left the police station and, as if in a trance, rode back to Pyefleet Manor.

XI

The day of the trial came upon them quickly. Lady Catherine hired a lawyer from London, a Mr. Ephraim Jaggett and he had busied himself for several days soliciting character references on Garrad's behalf from the staff at the manor and in the neighboring villages. He found them to be strangely taciturn, especially since Lady Catherine and Rose had said that Garrad was held in very high regard, both in his trade and in his person.

Rose told Mr. Jaggett that she believed that Sir Sydney and Squire Paxton had threatened everybody with punishment should they stand up for Garrad. At this Mr. Jaggett seemed to take umbrage.

"I am sure that these men you refer to are gentlemen. They would not resort to such infamy, such calumny," he puffed. "Preposterous! And now, if you please I must refresh myself," and with this he puffed and strode off to the pub, "The Donkey and Buskins."

Crestfallen, Rose walked back to the manor house where she found great agitation, with Travis setting Frederick upon an unsaddled horse. Tears were streaming down both their faces.

"What has happened?" asked Rose, already fearing the answer.

"Lady Catherine..." replied Travis. "She..."

"She suddenly took a terrible turn for the worse," interceded Mrs. Moffett. "'Twas but fifteen minutes ago. I took up her tea and she was gasping and gurgling so...her lungs filling with water, it seemed. I tried to lift her up to ease her breathing but she turned deathly pale and breathed her last, right in my arms. Terrible, it was." And she started to sob.

"Frederick," intervened Travis, having gained some composure, "Go and fetch Dr. Wickham."

"Yes sir," said Frederick who ran and mounted the readied horse in the stable yard and cantered, then galloped off.

"Where is Lady Charlotte?" asked Rose.

"Why, in her room, on her own. Where else?" ventured Mrs. Moffett, glancing over her shoulder to make sure her truthful utterance was not heard.

Rose was stunned. She was deeply saddened by the loss of her lady and friend but also had the sinking realization that there was no-one of influence to speak up for Garrad at his trial. Forlornly, with dragging steps, she wandered as if in a daze to the barn. She started to feel her mind clouding over as if a deep, black ooze was rising up from her depths. She then shivered with the fear that she might be going mad. There was no-one for her to talk to, to share her deep, dark lost self with.

As if she caught a sense of these deep troubling sentiments, Boudicca stirred and gently whinnied in her stall. Startled out of her reveries, Rose smiled to herself, finding humor in the fact that, at this moment of tragic loss and awful presentiments, Boudicca was to be her companion and confidant. She had always felt a deep affinity for this fine, recalcitrant, willful yet magnificent mare, perhaps because she always gave the "lord of the manor" such a difficult time. When he was with her, he could not be so high and mighty. Rose stepped over to Boudicca's stall and caressed her forehead. Then she hugged her bristly, warm neck that pulsated and throbbed with life. The very pulsation of life in the neck of the horse seemed to speak of a deep comforting wisdom and Rose felt herself calming down. Her thoughts strayed to Lady Catherine. She was no more. There would be no more afternoon readings, no more of her kind words and uplifting thoughts. Rose realized that she would have to take these experiences and enshrine them in her heart, mind and soul. She resolved to make a deliberate effort to remember all of the warmth of her relationship and to use these memories as a guide, as a support. She realized, as her bittersweet tears flowed down her cheeks and moistened the golden hairs on the Boudicca's neck, that she would always have a companion. "A telesphorus," she whispered to herself.

Boudicca, as if she realized that Rose had completed her rumination, stamped gently.

"Ah! I see, now you want your treat," said Rose. She fetched a handful of rolled oats and, holding her hand flat, watched Boudicca snuffle it up.

XII

Garrad's trial had brought out many onlookers. The court-house was full to overflowing. The constables came to Garrad's cell and led him to the ante room where Mr.

Jaggett, the lawyer, was waiting. As Garrad was roughly ushered into the room he thought he caught a glimpse of Mr. Jaggett quickly hiding a flask up his voluminous sleeve and then wiping his mouth,

"Ah, John m'boy!," he exclaimed.

"Garrad, sir…"

"Yes, yes, of course. Fear not my lad. Give not a whit of…er…well, let us just say, all will be well, as they say. Now, what shall be our defense?"

Garrad's heart sank as he saw his life at Pyefleet slip away from him. He smelled the gin on Jaggett's breath and could sense the chaos welling up around him. His head started to swim as he heard the crowd in the courtroom next door. With chilling clarity, he saw it all. Sir Sydney had accused him, enlisted the help of Squire Paxton and now had deliberately hired this incompetent sot to seal his fate. Lady Catherine had died. His life had come to an abrupt end.

He was led into the courtroom and he stood, as best he could, in the dock. Everything was swimming in front of him. Jaggett shuffled papers, misplaced documents and got lost in the proceedings. The judge became irate at his disorganization as one by one the witnesses came and went. Squire Paxton, speaking clearly and against Garrad and making it clear that Garrad was part of the rebellious movement that was sweeping the country, that Garrad was perhaps allied to the Irish and had been heard learning French. Garrad was precisely the kind of "rapscallion" that would have us end the monarchy, which had women and children trembling in their beds o'nights for fear of Boney. The judge and Jaggett seemed unable to stop these tirades which were amplified when Sir Sydney took the stand, praising his friend the Squire and complimenting the judge on his excellent hunting grounds. He reminded the judge of his contributions to the poor and needy of the Parish and again wondered aloud if "Hansen" might be an Irish name. Being Irish, of course, he would be sympathetic to the rebel cause and hostile to his masters. The prosecutor also referred to the loss of the American colonies some twenty-five years ago. It was leniency in the British Isles—threats of abolition, threats of reform, of giving the lower echelons the vote— this laxity had frightened the colonies and they had rebelled fearing that such looseness of command and punishment would result in insurrections and massacres—-no, he insisted, it was now time to reassure the people that the wave of insurrection, of unruliness stopped here and now. Hansen was to be used as an example of this reinstatement of the old order of things.

It took little of this to persuade the judge and he reached his decision quickly. Garrad was to be transported, to be taken to a prison hulk off Gravesend, held there until a transport ship would take him to Van Diemen's land, Australia.

Chapter 2

I

Garrad felt with his tongue the soft bloody space where once was his eye tooth. His left eye was half closed, swollen from the bludgeoning he had received in the gaol. He gazed out over the grey, slimy waters of the Thames estuary. Nearby a pair of gulls pecked and squawked over a dead fish washed up on the mudbank. The air was damp and chill.

"Heave to, me handsome lads!" croaked the trusty and Garrad and the dozen other prisoners carefully picked their way down the slippery seaweed strewn steps of the wharf. With their shackles clinking they settled down into the boat and the two oarsmen pulled them out to the prison-hulk, a retired battleship of the line used to house prisoners. For Garrad and his fellows, it would be their home until they were transferred to the ship that was to transport them to Australia or Van Diemen's Land.

As they cleared the jetty the icy east wind picked up and cut into the men. They saw their breath, even as they forged through the fog.

"Home at last, my beauties!" crowed the trusty. And he pointed through the mist to the daunting shadowy form of the hulk as it emerged from the mist. The oarsmen rowed on steadily as the swell seemed to pick up. Garrad was shivering with the cold. His body ached and his head ached, both from the beating and hunger. As they approached the sodden, overbearing mass of the prison hulk, the breeze carried to them its stench. All the men groaned in disgust as if they were one person.

"Make ready!" coughed the trusty, and a rope was thrown down from above-deck. Garrad looked up and noticed that the ship's name was "Liberty". Even in his abjection, he saw the humor, and smiled a private smile.

They were greeted on deck at the top of the makeshift steps by a leering swab brandishing a whip. The men were shoved below where the ceiling was so low Garrad had to almost crouch and was told to sit down on a wooden pallet, wet and stained with excrement and suppuration. The stench was so overpowering, his eyes watered and it was all he could do not to vomit. Several rats scampered boldly along the hatchway, fearless.

Finally their guardians went above and an eerie silence fell over the grim cabin.

"Which circle of hell do you take this for?" inquired a voice across the gangway.

Garrad looked up and was greeted by a pair of eyes that looked as if they had been gouged out of rock, and a smile that revealed blackened and yellowed teeth. He found himself wondering how anyone familiar with Dante could find themselves in such a situation. Then he realized he had but to look in a mirror for an answer.

"One near the center, I'll warrant," replied Garrad. "Though it is strange indeed to be here for the supposed theft of six-pennyworth of pheasant."

"You are from Essex?" inquired this stranger. "I can hear your accent."

"Indeed, on the Pyefleet Channel," replied Garrad.

"Ah! Excellent—cockles, winkles, and, of course, oysters."

"You know the place?"

"I know those waters like the back of my hand. That is where I was caught. They took me for a smuggler, bringing contraband up the creeks to the Peldon duck pond."

Garrad was flabbergasted. He had heard stories since he was a lad of the smugglers hiding their contraband in the depths of the duck pond in nearby Peldon, right outside the pub, and here was one, sitting in shackles right across from him. Garrad smiled at the irony.

There was a moment of silence as Garrad let this story sink in. Finally, the man broke the silence. "You will need a friend in this hell-hole. I suggest we become mates. Foxglove is the name."

"On the strength of Dante and Essex?"

"Aye on that very strength," asserted Foxglove and with a rattle of his chains and wincing at the pain of his cuffs, he reached across to Garrad. They shook hands.

II

Several days and nights passed by on the hulk. The incessant rocking, the slop, the damp and the constant groaning and yelling of the men wore Garrad down until he felt he was losing his grasp of time and place. Day and night swum together in a delirious fetid smog and dreams, nightmares and the brutal realities of the hulk all intertwined. He felt as though he was slipping into madness. The only thing that kept him sane was his new friend Foxglove who seemed blessed with high spirits and would determinedly engage Garrad in conversations to pass the time. Fatigued as they were, they discussed anything—places they had been, horses they had known and the people they missed. Foxglove noticed that Garrad was uncannily silent when the memory of Rose came to the fore and he sensitively and judiciously veered the conversation to a lighter topic.

There were several unfortunate madmen on the hulk. They would rant and rave and talk to imaginary others at all hours. There were also some very stony fellows who said little but whose piercing gazes spoke of cruelty in volumes.

Garrad took a liking to several robust Irishmen who were perhaps there simply for voicing some sentiment in favor of independence of their nation or of the changes afoot in France; perhaps simply for being Irish in the wrong place and at the wrong time. Occasionally, they would muster their spirits enough to sing a rebel song or a lament for their lost land or loved ones. They seemed to take pleasure when this would bring about the ire of their sullen keepers above-deck.

Despite these diversions, Garrad could feel his body and mind wasting away for want of food, sleep, warmth and, most of all the love of his Rose. At times he would try to sustain his faded spirits by closing his eyes and imagining himself with her—on the beach by the Red Crag, counting linnets as they walked down Oliver's Lane, gathering bluebells in Friday Woods, wading in the crisp riffling waters of Bounstead Brook—but more often than not, these reveries would be sharply terminated with a tirade from one of his benighted fellows storming out in a mad rage or the sound of someone vomiting, or cursing.

Some small relief from this cramped torture came when, on about the seventh day, they were dragged above and transferred to the ship that was to take them to Australia. Garrad and his fellows made a sorry sight, especially when compared to the sailors aboard the ship they were being transferred to. As they prepared the ship they were singing.

> "In South Australia, I was born,
> Heave away, haul away!
> South Australia, round Cape Horn,
> You're bound for South Australia!"

Even in his depleted, miserable state, Garrad caught the irony, as did Foxglove. As they lined up on their new ocean-going ship, the Captain paraded up and down in front of them.

"My name is Martins!" he proclaimed, "and I am your nemesis and master! Woe betide you if you do not obey me in the coming months. I have a cat! Not a pet but a whip. I have a rope, long enough for keel hauling. Yes sir! Disobey me and I shall haul you under the beam of the ship. A merry sight indeed sir!" and as if to prove his point he walked up to one of the men who had started, in his fear to rave.

"You, sir! I shall have your name!"

"John Baptist, or so I am called by my liege, for I have done no wrong. The butter was mine!"

Martins turned and addressed the entire ship. "You see? We shall have none of this. Scudder! Beat this man!"

At this command a lean, lanky ensign unhooked a lead-filled cosh from his belt and set about the John the Baptist who started to rave even more, squealing like a baby while the men about him, still chained to him, recoiled.

"Enough! Enough medicine for the wretch. He shall soon get better with this poultice! Hah!" exclaimed Martins, seemingly enlivened, braced by the beating. Scudder re-hooked his cosh to his belt.

"Below with them! We have our full complement. We sail this evening with the tide," commanded Martins and the men were led shuffling below, dragging John the Baptist, who was beaten, bloody and barely able to stand. Below they were chained to the bulkhead on damp straw mattresses that were to be their homes for the next months.

That evening the anchor was weighed and, with a stiff, cold, following breeze, the ship forged its way down the channel. Conditions below decks worsened as men vomited and gagged with the incessant heaving of the ship in the swell and chop, the waves slapping against the oaken hull, sometimes with a shuddering, deafening thump. The night was long, cold and putrid. Garrad could not sleep for the agitation so he calmed his mind by imagining himself back home—a summer's day by Bounstead brook, he and Rose, hand in hand—he would make her a chain of daisies and crown her with it. They would catch sticklebacks and elvers with a fishnet—it was there he learned how to swim—on and on he pressed his thoughts and memories, as if to hold his mind together with love—love of place and person.

Others were not so fortunate. Foxglove was wracked with bellyache and the poor soul who called himself John the Baptist and had received a coshing was raving at the top of his lungs, barely intelligible since his lips and gums were so swollen.

"Cast forth, am I upon this ship of fools....denizens of the deep...madmen who cannot see their way...baptism... saviour..." he cried out, finally collapsing into inconsolable weeping which only further drew the curses and threats from the others.

They rolled back and forth thus all night, hoping for some mercy as dawn broke. But the morning was grey and chill and the thin gruel that was slopped out before them cold also.

"Eat up, my hearties!" cried out the coxswain. "You will need your strength for the Celtic Sea, I'll warrant." And he laughed mirthlessly.

And so they all lay there, in chains, for two more days until finally the stench became too overwhelming for even those above deck and they were dragged above, leaving several men behind to clean up the waste that had accumulated.

As they stepped above, the cold clean air of the Bay of Biscay smacked Garrad in the face like the snap of a wet towel, and awoke his spirit. With pleasure he allowed his eyes to scan the horizon. For days they had only been able to see a few feet ahead in the gloom below.

Suddenly Scudder cried out. "Whale! Beaked Whale!" And he ran and grabbed his flintlock from the armory and aimed and shot at the beast as it breeched. He reloaded, waited, laughed and then shot again as the beast surfaced for air once again.

At this John Baptist, who had been one of those left behind to clean below, came above carrying a filthy armful of straw. He saw Scudder shooting at the whale and became transported with grief and rage.

"My mother! My mother! You shoot my mother! No! This cannot be. You must cease, cease! Vengeance!" and he ran across deck, for they had released him from his shackles so he could clean more easily. With one swoop he clutched on to Scudder and with a strength that seemed to come from the depths of his being, lifted him up and they both tumbled overboard. Garrad was stabbed to the core by the look of terror in Scudder's eyes. He knew in that moment that he was locked in an embrace of death with John Baptist. His hand clutched at the rail, turned white, and then gave way as they plunged out of sight.

"Man overboard! Man overboard!" cried out several sailors, but it was no use. The ship forged on, still with a following wind. They looked astern, but no sign of the two could be seen.

"Hard about sir?" asked one of the midshipmen of the captain.

The captain simply turned forward, turned up the collar of his coat and with a nod gestured full ahead. Garrad and Foxglove exchanged glances with expressions that conveyed sadness for old John Baptist and deep astonishment at the entire event. They were careful not to reveal any pleasure they might have taken in Scudder's fate.

III

It was so dark below where the men were held that day and night blended together in an eternal grim twilight. Some of the men seemed to lapse into a comatose state. Others writhed in pain, groaning, holding their bellies. Yet others wept inconsolably. Some stared into space.

Garrad and Foxglove chose to pass the time in conversation that would take their minds off of their sorry plight. Deeply fatigued and wracked with belly ache though they were, they forced utterances at a slow deliberate pace, motivated by the idea that this was their rebellion, their mutiny.

"Horses," started Garrad. "I live and breathe horses. I can tell what is on their mind just by running my hand over their flanks."

"I am that way with a stream," responded Foxglove. "I can hear it breathe and tell where there are fish."

"Sometimes a horse will tremble in such a way as to let you know what is in its soul," mused Garrad, not quite sure where his thoughts were coming from, "and if you listen, you will know just how much you can ask of her."

"Mmm…" responded Foxglove. "I love to catch dace. They love the clean, fast water. I use long trotting to snare them. Beautiful silver fish!"

"Ah, yes," responded Garrad. "Now a charger, there is a horse for you…"

…and so they continued, each musing aloud in the presence of the other, feeling no constraint to respond, just gaining some comfort from the reminiscence and having it witnessed by the other.

"The birds you see," started Foxglove, "my favorite is the Avocet, so graceful with its upcurving bill…."

"Aye, but the Sheld Duck…"

"A handsome bird…"

…and so they continued, sustaining pleasant memories for as long as they could, until, overcome by deep fatigue, they fell asleep.

IV

The heat became more oppressive and the stench below deck got thicker with each passing day. The slop they were served more and more resembled the vomit they had witnessed but a short time earlier. The crew that brought them their victuals seemed to derive pleasure from the squalor the convicts endured.

"Cheer up mateys! The Horse Latitudes are nigh!" said Scunthorpe, in his strange gargling voice. "We will spend enough time there. Feel her!" he said pointing upwards, meaning that they were to sense the ship. "See, it's like she knows we will be becalmed. Nothing but the still sea." And with that he ascended through the hatchway.

As Scunthorpe had predicted, the ship was becalmed. He had not predicted however that Captain Martins, with little to do but wait for a breeze, was to go mad, perhaps aided by rum, perhaps simply from underemployment. The Horse Latitudes are so named because too often, ships, becalmed in the still air, would run out of water and the horse would be the first to die of thirst. It would then be eaten or its rotting carcasses thrown overboard. There were no horses on Garrad's ship but one of the ensigns, after raving for several days finally succumbed to fever and his yellowed body was summarily thrown overboard by several of the convicts. This seemed to unhinge Martins, for he started talking about his son who had been lost in a naval action with the French. He took to drinking and at night raved up and down the decks, brandishing his sword at imaginary foes, issuing orders to fire away. Calm only came when, exhausted, he fell into a deep sleep in a rope locker, where he lay until the next mad paroxysm overtook him. The days wore on, the sea flat and oily in the dead calm.

"Come on mateys," yelled Scunthorpe. "Come up for air, scum that you are." And so all the convicts stumbling in their chains, squinting in the unaccustomed light were lead and dragged above deck.

"I'll need two of you to clean out below deck. You and you." And with this he pointed out Foxglove and Bailey who were unchained and given a shovel and a swab-mop to clean out the diseased mulch in which the convicts had been laying for days. Garrad was relieved, since this was the most nauseating of tasks. He did, however, give Foxglove, his fast friend, a sympathetic glance.

The men stood, half dazed, half propping each other up as they took in as much fresh air as they could while the muck was cleaned out below. This was a welcome respite, from the tortures and utter boredom below deck. Finally, Foxglove and Bailey had finished shoveling and swabbing and they sagged their way up to the open air. At that very moment Martins, who had been sleeping in the nearest footlocker awoke and saw them. He must have thought, in his madness, that they were carrying not shovel and broom, but weapons, for he immediately drew his sabre and exclaimed, "Avast! Mutiny! Scunthorpe! Apprehend them! In irons with them"

Foxglove and Bailey were dazzled by the light, fatigued and confused, so they just stood there, stunned. Scunthorpe however, readily obeyed and with the aid of two of his fellows quickly placed the irons around the two supposed mutineers.

"Rope. Prepare them for hauling!" bellowed Martins, brandishing his sabre, swooning and convulsing.

"Aye, aye captain," replied Scunthorpe as he gestured to two deckhands to get ropes ready.

As they secured the ropes around Foxglove and Bailey's waists Garrad blurted out, "Not keel-hauling! They could die from that! And they did nothing."

Martins stiffened and seemed to sober as he fixed his watery gaze on Garrad, "Aye, sir, keel hauling. They shall be dragged under the boat, one side to the other. Double! A double keel hauling!" It was as if the idea came to him suddenly. "Scunthorpe, they shall be hauled at once. And take this scum if he utters one more word."

"Aye, captain," replied Scunthorpe, with a smile. And the shackles were removed from Bailey and Foxglove as they were led up to forward so the ropes could be looped under the prow. Then carefully, step by step they were lead abaft to the center-deck where each man was held by a rope that went under the entire ship and up the other side where it was held by a deckhand.

"Let us have three at each rope, Mr. Scunthorpe. Teach these lubbers how we deal with disobedience and talk of mutiny," slurred Martins.

"Aye, captain," and three deckhands grabbed each of the ropes.

"Your life, in their hands," said Martins to Bailey and Foxglove. "The way of the sea. Pray that they pull you hard and fast, or 'twill be a long journey for you. Hah!"

"Breathe fast and deep," called out Garrad to the two men. Bailey seemed to have fainted, for his legs gave way and he had to be supported to the edge of the boat.

"Good luck lads!"

"Hold fast, boys," came encouraging remarks from those prisoners who knew what was about to happen.

"Shove and heave ho!" declaimed Martins and at this deckhands pushed and bundled both Foxglove and Bailey over the edge of the ship and immediately the other deckhands heaved on the ropes.

"Heave, one! Heave ho!" they called in a unison that surprised Garrad, for it seemed as if they had done this many times before. Garrad found himself holding his breath, as if to identify with Foxglove, his friend. After about five pulls of the rope he calculated that the men were about half way under the ship. His breath was still holding, so he reckoned that Foxglove and Bailey, if they kept their wits, would last until they were pulled up the other side.

But at precisely this point, the men tugged but the ropes did not give. They tugged again but the ropes remained taut.

"They are caught, Captain. Snagged. Perhaps in each other," Scunthorpe reported to Martins.

"Uhuh," the captain replied, for he seemed to have drifted off and seemed oblivious to what was happening. "Then pull harder, swabs," he cried out, as if in a dream.

"Aye, captain. Pull boys! Pull!"

And the men pulled and pulled. Garrad felt his breath and chest tightening as he realized he had run out of breath. The wind picked up, riffling the milky-grey ocean and causing the sails to flap and the sheets to sting against the masts, reminding Garrad of Pyefleet. As he came back to his senses, he realized it was too long, far too long. Bailey and Foxglove had become entangled under the ship, perhaps because Bailey had passed out. Foxglove had struggled, but to no avail.

The hands kept pulling and tugging, changing their positions to perhaps release the two, but to no avail.

"Let go the ropes, sir?" inquired Scunthorpe of Martins.

"What? Yes, what you will. I'll to my cabin," replied Martins. "Take them below. Use this breeze sir, to good effect!"

"Aye, captain" replied Scunthorpe. The men released the ropes that ploshed into the sea and set about trimming the sails. As the ship started to make some headway, Garrad and his fellows shuffled below decks to their straw beds.

Chapter 3

I

Sheets of grey rain swept across the Pyefleet Channel. Swirls of mists eddied over the marshes. The world seemed to fall into an eternal twilight. Rose had been in her bed for several days, sleeping, immobile and refusing to eat. Frederick, the stable boy, had taken the new kittens to see if they would enliven her spirit. Mrs. Moffet had taken her a serving of steaming rabbit stew but all this was to no avail.

Rose had been in a tormented inner frenzy. Grief, in all of its many forms, had been washing over her, keeping her from sleep and from any repose, quietude or stillness. She was assailed by the strangest images. She had seen humble bees die after delivering their sting, since the sting took with it an essential part of their body. In losing Garrad she felt as though a vital part of her flesh had been torn from her, and now she was inexorably wasting away. She recalled Donne's poem about midwinter, how she likened his grief to the sap in the trees sinking down to the very roots. That was how she felt. The sap was her once vibrant soul and it had shrunk. It had left her eyes, her face, her heart, torso and legs. It had sunk deep into the ground beneath her feet, never to be retrieved. She became frightened, for she knew this was her life-force leaving her. She was as the walking dead on All Soul's Night. Then again, a wave of rage would wash over her like a rogue wave such as they had on the banks offshore. She would grind her teeth and pull at her hair, contorting her body in anguish. She felt herself becoming enraged at herself for having loved so much, so deeply, reasoning that if she had not loved so, she would not feel such excruciating agonies. "Never again!" she would utter to herself, but then she would realize that this was the speech of someone who had given up on life, who was consigning themselves to a half-life of purgatorial mediocrity.

She felt herself sinking lower and lower into despair and at each lowering she felt, paradoxically, less of the pain of loss, but more of the fear of dying. Finally, as she felt herself sink even further into the grey forlornness, she had a strange vision. Staring into grey nothingness, her vision constricted and her body aching, she slipped into a hypnagogic state—half awake, half dreaming—and a silhouette hovered above her. It was a woman, and she emanated nothing but love, warmth, concern and tenderness. Rose had no conscious memory of her mother but, without hesitation or any forethought, knew that this was she. Later, she would be uncertain as to whether this had been a visitation or the recovery of a loving tender memory from before she could recall. Nonetheless, this image, hovering over her and then reaching out a consoling, comforting hand was enough to make Rose brim up and overflow with the deepest sense of gratitude. She felt her heart swell again, and as it swelled there was a pinch of half-pleasurable pain, for it had grown accustomed over the past days to being shrunken. But now it swelled, and, as it swelled, so Rose breathed deeply. The vision went away. Rose looked around the room. It looked different. The colours were brighter, the edges sharper. It was as if part of her had come back to life. She sighed, and started to ponder this strange transformative experience.

Just then, she heard a chaise draw up outside the house. Someone had arrived. It was her sister, Kitty, who had been making daily visits since the twin catastrophes.

II

"She is like a ghost since Garrad's fate, and then, of course, she and Lady Catherine were soul-mates," Mrs. Moffett explained to Kitty as she shook off the rain from her topcoat.

"I shall try again and see if I can bring some life into her, for she is too young to pine away so," replied Kitty as she made her way up the narrow staircase to Rose's room.

"God bless you my dear, for who knows how long his lordship will put up with her being abed so."

Kitty entered Rose's room and sat on the bed. "Rose, my dear. This will not do. We must be about something. You must not simply waste away. I will not lose my only friend in this cruel world." And she took hold of Rose's wan hand and rubbed it as if to bring her to life. Rose looked slowly at her friend and then resumed her vacant staring at the ceiling.

Kitty was at a loss as to what she might do next. She glanced around the room, as if looking for something that would stimulate a conversation and bring her friend back to life. On the wall was a picture of an old Essex sailing barge, ploughing through the rough seas off the Dogger Bank. Rose had won it as a prize singing at the parish fete.

"We should go sailing when the weather improves!" she suddenly burst out. "When the weather improves," she added. "It will bring fresh life to your cheek!" Then Kitty, realizing the foolishness of her outburst, slumped down, for it seemed yet another attempt at bringing some cheer to her friend had failed.

But suddenly Rose started. She blinked, as if an idea had come to her. Kitty, alarmed said, "What is it?"

Rose did not answer but it was apparent that something was stirring in her. She put her finger to her chin, as if pondering and then said, "I have it. That is what I shall do… we, if you will accompany me." And she turned to Kitty with a light in her eyes, a light that Kitty had not seen for far too many days.

"What are you saying?"

"I am saying that I, or we, if you wish to accompany me, will sail to Australia to retrieve my lost love." Rose said this firmly and steadily.

"A joke, I am sure, my dear, for you…"

"No. No, I have the wherewithal. Lady Catherine gave me money. More than enough for both of us, look!" With this, Rose, with sudden animation, slid out of bed and retrieved the purse from under it. She opened it and displayed the contents, bills endorsed by the bank of England.

"What do you say?"

"This is insanity," replied Kitty. "Besides, my father…I am sorry…"

"I am going," said Rose resolutely. "But you must tell no-one, not even your father, at least, not until after I am gone. I do not want anyone to dissuade me. I will leave this coming Saturday. Ships leave from Portsmouth. I will visit you Friday at tea-time and that will have to be our secret farewell."

"Oh Rose, this is insanity…are you sure?"

"I must. I feel as though part of my very body is missing. I know I will go to the grave early if I am not with my Garrad. And I know that he holds out hope to be with me and that is keeping him alive." Then, looking about the room, "I must think of what I shall need."

"I shall help you."

III

Next morning, Rose and Mrs. Moffett were busy washing the dishes after breakfast, their faces beaded with perspiration and their hands red from the scalding water and soap. Mrs. Moffett would have it no other way in her kitchen.

"Where is that Molly? She is such a scatterbrain! She was supposed to be here to help with these dishes and look, we are almost done and no sign of her," exclaimed the frustrated Mrs. Moffett. Rose smiled to herself but no sooner was this said and done than Molly herself, tearful and red-eyed stepped in the kitchen with her father, Dan Pritchett who himself had a tear streaked face, firm mouth and tight jutting jaw.

"Tell'em! Go on, tell 'em! I want all the world to know," he muttered through gritted teeth, nudging Molly forward. "Go on!"

"I'm havin' a baby," Molly finally managed to bring forth.

"What?" exclaimed Mrs Moffett.

"But how…" asked Rose. Molly hadn't even a boy courting her.

"Tell 'em! Tell 'em who the father is! I want everyone to know, before I cut him down with my scythe," blurted out Dan, barely containing his rage and tears.

"The squire," mumbled Molly.

"Yes. The squire, that poxy cur," exploded Dan. Rose and Mrs. Moffett gestured to calm Dan down and moved in to comfort the now weeping Molly.

"She was coming home across Gorse Fields. Been gathering blackberries. Innocent as the day is long, my little girl," and at this he could contain himself no more and fell to weeping uncontrollably.

"Oh my goodness, do sit down Molly," said Mrs. Moffett, "and you too Dan. We shall sort this mess out."

"I shall sort him out! I shall slice him up and feed him to my pigs!"

"And then who will take care of Molly?" asked Mrs. Moffett. "You know you are all she has got. Let us be prudent. Things have a way of working out. Right now, we need to comfort Molly. And you must be careful not to bandy this about. You know how vengeful they can be. It will be trouble for you, perhaps for all of us."

"I shall have my due justice," said Dan "and Molly too."

"Yes I believe you shall, Mr. Pritchett," said Rose comfortingly.

"Why don't you two sit down there, by the nook, and I shall get to work. Molly, I think you should tell Rose all about it, as it will ease your mind of the terrible burden you are bearing," said Mrs. Moffett.

"Thank you," said Rose gently as she ushered the distraught Molly to the seats in the kitchen nook. Molly told her how she had been walking back across the Gorse fields after having found some early blackberries. She was going to make a pie. Suddenly, squire Paxton rides up, gets off his horse and starts commenting on how she has grown, how pretty she looked and so on. Then he started making improper advances and despite her protestations he continued. Finally, at the end, he got very angry, as if she was doing something wrong by telling him not to touch her, and he just kept on. At this Molly could say no more as she broke down into inconsolable sobs. She had not wanted to tell anybody, for she felt such shame and felt sure that everyone would say she was lying and no good, but finally, her mother couldn't help but notice a certain broadening of her hips and asked at which point Molly finally broke down. Then her father came home and he, of course threatened to go and kill the squire. Molly begged to be brought over to the manor house, and here she was, terrified, ashamed and distraught beyond recognition.

"I know, my dear. You are stretched beyond your wit's end."

"I shall have my way with him, I swear!" interjected Dan "Such an outrage, such a disgrace! I have no recourse. You know how they are. They stick together like limpets. I feel I shall burst."

"Wait one minute," said Rose, and she went to her room. In a few minutes she returned with an envelope which she gave to Molly.

"Here, take this. It will help cover whatever costs you may have to bear in the coming months and years. No. Do not worry. It is not a large amount, and I can well afford it. I have been putting some money aside for quite some time. Just do not bruit it about. I know it will not heal one one-hundredth of what needs healing, but perhaps it will help."

"God bless you, Rose," whispered Molly, through her tears.

"And keep you," chimed in Dan.

IV

It wrenched Rose's heart to say goodbye to Mrs. Moffett, Travis, Frederick and all the others at the house as if she was just going for tea with Kitty, when she knew that this was farewell, probably forever. She knew, however, that if she told them the truth of her intentions there would be much ado. Lady Charlotte and Sir Sydney would intercede and stop her somehow. She stifled her tears, waved a last goodbye and set out down the sea wall to the vicarage.

She had sewn the money cleverly into the lining of her large carpet-bag and left it the previous night hidden under the lych-gate. She retrieved it and slung it over her shoulder on the way to Kitty's house.

The tea with Kitty and her parents was equally straining on her composure as she made small talk, for in the back of her mind, she knew that she would soon be leaving.

She was jarred however, when Parson Highweather mentioned that two men from the Admiralty had visited last week with questions about any strange visitor in the area since intelligence had it that some Frenchmen had been seen scouting the coast and inlets. Oddly, added the Parson, these inquiries had involved Squire Paxton and Sir Sydney. "A rum business, I'm sure," opined the Parson.

When the sun had dropped low over the wheat-fields and the last tea-cake had been eaten, Kitty said, "I shall walk you to the sea wall, Rose."

When they got to the sea wall, they embraced, both tearing up. Kitty gave Rose a necklace with a locket containing her picture. "So you don't forget, your sister," she almost gasped, so strong was her emotion.

"I shall never forget you. I feel we shall meet again one day. I must go."

And with that Rose set off down the sea wall, away from the manor, towards Peldon where she would catch the evening coach to Maldon.

V

She arrived in Maldon in time to purchase sundries and lodged for the night in the Greene King, overlooking the quay, which was bustling even at this late hour as the herring-boats readied for the next morning.

"Could any of these boats be enlisted to take me to Portsmouth?" she inquired of the innkeeper.

"Portsmouth, you say," replied the man, stroking his beard. "I will not ask you why such a lady as yourself would want to undertake such a journey....but Ned over there would be your man."

Rose looked across the room and in the amber, smoky light discerned a hunched, grey- bearded fellow, nursing a pint pot and musing with a clay pipe.

"Agreed," said the innkeeper, "Not much to behold. But as fine a sailor the Essex coast ever saw. Too old for fishing, but he undertakes a long journey, every now and then." And at this the innkeeper stroked his nose and winked, implying that Ned might have truck with contraband. Rose knew enough to ignore this imputation.

"Would you be so kind as to introduce me?"

"Of course, milady!" replied the innkeeper.

The innkeeper went over to Ned who nodded several times. Returning, the innkeeper said, "Ned agrees and says the tide runs well at five tomorrow morning. Meet him by the door, over there."

Rose looked across the room at Ned and they briefly nodded at each other, as if to seal the deal. Her heart was fluttering, but her will was firm. She also felt a strange exaltation at the freedom she glimpsed as she stepped into the unknown.

VI

The following morning skeins of fine mist had rolled in off the North Sea. Ned, hunched under several heavy blankets, gestured for her to follow him down the jetty to his boat. A small, scruffy boy sat wanly by the tiller.

"We never discussed your price," said Rose.

"Florins will do," gruffly replied Ned.

Unsure as to how many, Rose felt in her purse and handed him five. He looked at them in his palm, pocketed them and tugged at his forelock in thanks. Ned grunted and offered his hand to assist Rose onto the boat, "The Mary Lee" and she sat on the damp bench amidships.

In silence they set sail into the grey mist and waters. Soon a chop picked up, the breeze stiffened out of the northeast and Rose felt the thrill of excitement and dread as the boat picked up speed and started smacking into the waves.

The sun faintly gleamed through the mist after an hour or so and Rose gratefully felt some of its warmth. Ned pulled a loaf out of his sack and broke off a piece for her and offered her to share his bottle of tea. All the time the boy attended to the tiller and the sheets, keeping them taut and straining.

"You shall need this," offered Ned as he handed Rose a thick horse-blanket. "We make good time. By nightfall we shall be in the channel."

Rose wrapped herself in the blanket, which indeed still smelled of horses, reminding her poignantly of her Garrad, and she willed herself into a doze.

As night fell and they turned west into the channel, the wind and the waves picked up. The boat seemed to race, creak and strain, but Ned and the boy remained calm so Rose felt that she should not worry, despite the stinging salt spray that would waken her at every other turn.

Mercifully, the wind and waves abated and Rose drifted off to sleep. At dawn the grey lines of the south coast of England stood off to the right. Ned was at the tiller and the boy was curled up asleep in the rope-locker.

"Morning, miss," said Ned brightly. "Breakfast is at your side." And Rose turned to see that, yes indeed, there was a bottle of tea, a hunk of bread and a square of hard-tack on the bench beside her. Trying not to feel forlorn, she chewed at her meal, reflecting that this, for Ned, was as fine a day as could be expected. She scoured her mind for ways of keeping up her spirits.

Ned, seeming to sense her flagging spirits, said, "Portsmouth is just around the headland, miss."

Rose teared up at his unexpected kindness for it seemed he had read her sentiments exactly. She took a swig of the tea, and settled herself in the warmth of the horse-blanket for the rest of the journey.

Unsure as to whether it would help her mood or cause her more pain, Rose finally decided to conjure up memories of the past. She found that while they were bittersweet as she compared these past delights to her present situation, on balance they helped her mood and strengthened her resolve to see this through. She recalled scenes from childhood—learning to swim in Bounstead Brook, in the crisp dappled waters, seemingly surrounded by sinuous, black elvers and shimmering, darting sticklebacks—gathering cockles out on the mudflats of the channel at low tide, how they would crouch down and wait for the cockle to send up its tell-tale squirt and then finding the slightly darker hue of mud where, some inches below, there lurked the fat ivory and chrome yellow streaked mollusk—holding hands with Garrad while gathering blackberries, their fingers stained blue, purple and black as if they were scriveners, the sun beating on them so hard they became drowsy. At this she herself became drowsy and fell asleep.

She awoke and they were enveloped by a clinging grey miasma. The sea was still choppy and slapped against the side of the boat. Rose smiled at the scrawny boy who had fallen asleep himself. Ned was at the tiller and he nodded, almost cheerfully at Rose who then peered into the fog.

After hour after endless hour of grey-slapping sea, crusts, tea and hard-tack, Rose felt the boat shift in direction. She roused herself from the mesmerized state she had adapted to dull the fatigue and boredom and looked up.

"Yes, miss. Portsmouth. Safe and sound."

And she could see in the gathering light the masts of the ocean-going vessels, one of which she would probably be boarding for Australia. As they approached, she heard the tintinnabulation of the harbor–tinkling of bells, creaking of wet timber, whistles, the screeching of herring-gulls—all the wonderful sounds of the land. She breathed deeply and felt her resolve and her spirits return.

VII

Her ship, "The Esmeralda" seemed to bounce out of Portsmouth harbor and into the west channel where the rhythm of the waves' chop met the counterpoint of the ocean swell. Rose attempted to settle her stomach on two accounts; the first was in simple reaction to the heaving of the sea for this was far more than she had ever experienced in her occasional jaunts around the estuary in a borrowed skiff with Garrad. The second had to do with the dread she felt at venturing into the unknown, unaccompanied. This she met with the acknowledgment she made to herself that she had no choice. It was as if there was a cord tied around her heart that joined her to Garrad. She must respond to its tugging or they both would simply waste away.

The ship seemed to beat and pound its way down the English Channel all day. Almost at every wave it felt to Rose as if the timbers were being stricken by a huge rock that shook the entire vessel and all on it to their bones.

The ship was on its way to supply the settlements in Australia. What with the strong headwind, there was much to occupy the sailors so they had little time to wonder at why a woman alone should be embarking on such a trip. She found that, apart from three stern hopefuls and would-be adventurers seeking a better life in Australia, she was alone among the passengers. Rose preferred it this way, for she needed time to compose her thoughts and feelings and to reflect upon the task she had set herself.

Night fell and she retired to her cabin, which seemed more to her like a recently converted locker, furnished with a rude bench upon which lay a lumpy kapok mattress and several blankets. She slept fitfully, troubled as she was by the racing thoughts and the overwhelming sense of void that settled upon her. These sentiments were soon dissipated, however as the grim light of dawn crept across the sea and the sky and they started to sail into the heavy swells of the Bay of Biscay. She braced herself against the closed-in walls of her cabin as the ship rolled and lurched and lifted and slammed down on the cresting waves. Above, she could hear the frenzied movement and shouts of the sailors as they went about securing the ship from capsizing. As the sea became even rougher and the wind screamed even louder, she found herself gripping on so tight that her fingernails started to blanch and give her pain. She wanted to cover her ears and crawl into a small space as if to deny what was happening all around her. Then, suddenly, without warning, without any forethought or willing, she found herself at peace. It was as if she had discovered a small space deep inside her soul where all was calm. From this space, she could with absolute calm survey the situation she was in, accept it, show concern for it, but not be possessed by it. She struggled for words to capture this new experience. Finally she said to herself, "I am in this storm, but I am not possessed by it."

And so, in this newly discovered frame of mind, she rode through the storm, which continued for several hours, marveling at this new discovery, feeling liberated and empowered by its import.

At noon, a sailor, drenched, shivering and exhausted came to her door with a flagon of beer and some tack, which she gratefully ate, feeling thankful that she was not suffering from *mal de mer*, as she could hear some of her fellow travellers were.

As late afternoon slowly turned into early evening, she thought she could feel some abatement in the ferocity of the waves and the same sailor returned and reported to her and the other passengers.

"Cape Finisterre off the port bow. Calmer seas ahead!"

VIII

It had been two full days since the troubled crossing of the Bay of Biscay and the weather was fine with a clear blue sky and sparkling waves. Rose climbed up on deck and surveyed with squinting eyes the crisp blue air and vast blue firmament. She breathed deeply, as if finally relaxing after the dread she had experienced in the past days, recapturing, by dint of will the calm space she had discovered in the grip of the storm.

"A fine morning, milady!" called out Captain Piggott from the deck.

"It is indeed, captain," replied Rose. And she sat down and leaned back on the rope-locker, closing her eyes as if to drink in the sun.

No sooner had she done so than there came the call from the crow's nest above.

"Three lateens off the port, captain."

As if galvanized, the captain took up his telescope and surveyed the port horizon. Snapping it shut he yelled out, "Full sail, full sail ahead."

"Full sail it is captain," came the series of responses as the crew swiftly set about hauling the sheets. Rose had to move as the men needed the very ropes she was reclining on.

"Aye, miss, I am afraid we are in for a chase, for they are Barbary Corsairs, as sure as I am captain."

Rose had heard of these ships, and once again she felt dread clench at her chest.

"Will they catch us?" she inquired.

"They are fast, to be sure. We shall do our best."

Only dimly comforted by this response, Rose stepped up to the edge and peered into the deceptively peaceful blue. After some minutes of straining, she finally saw three smudges, just this side of the horizon, each smudge comprised of three triangles. Those she concluded must be the lateen sails that she had heard of in stories of the Berber Pirates. She had been told that they captured and enslaved those on board, selling the women to wealthy men and the men as laborers. Thinking this, she took a deep breath and attempted to sense if the ship on which she was sailing had miraculously picked up speed.

Captain Piggott, seeming to pick up on her distress, called out, "We shall do our best miss, though it will be a long day!"

And a long day it was, and forlorn, for despite the strength of her wishes otherwise, the smudges grew bigger and the terrible, graceful triangles of the corsair's sails grew more distinct by the hour. The men took to praying and crossing themselves with more frequency and their handling of the sheets and sails and rigging became more and more urgent, as if the slightest error could change their fate, their entire lives.

Night fell and all were told to give off no light, not so much as a pipe, for fear that the corsairs would sight them. The occasional star peeping through the clouds allowed Piggott to aim due south, hoping to reach the safety of Lisbon or Gibraltar. All through the night the men did their work communicating only in whispers or gestures, secretly praying that when dawn broke, the horizons would be clear of the pirate's sails.

As dawn broke slowly, all eyes peered into the lifting grey for signs of the corsairs. Eventually again came the cry from the crow's nest above, "Lateens off the starboard!" And it was as if a tremor shot through the entire ship, for there, only a mile away were the three sets of sails of the corsairs.

"That's it me boys!" called out the captain. "We have nothing but a brace of five pounders, half a dozen muskets and sabres. We can die here fighting or hope for better times ahead." The men, disconsolate and exhausted did not quarrel with Piggott, although Rose was filled with deep dread at what this might mean for her.

And so it was that by noon the three boats had heaved alongside and taken over the ship, gleeful and exuberant at the ease with which they took their spoils. The leader, draped in orange finery and baggy pantaloons, bearing a scimitar, ordered the men below and with ease assigned his henchmen to take over the ship as if it was their own. Rose was treated as a special prize, as the leader circled around her, sizing her up as if she were a show horse. This of course discomforted her greatly, but she was lead to the captain's quarters where two of the corsairs were assigned to keep a close watch on her.

All four boats then headed south, in the direction they had been pursuing. They brought Rose food and she passed the next few days in this confinement. The men confined below were silent, probably from despair, defeat and fear. At least, Rose reasoned, since they were all to be slaves there would be little wish to do them harm, since they were chattel for sale. Damaged goods would not reach such a high price in the market-place. These musings provided her some cold comfort as she heard the strange language amongst the pirates as they managed their new ship in the gathering breeze.

IX

Rose awoke from a sleep that was mercifully dreamless. The men brought her foods that were strange, odd balls of mush and mint teas.

"al ribat. al ribat!" they said to her, pointing ahead. She gathered that they were referring to their destination and that they would be there soon. All seemed to be in good humor. She surmised that this was because they had made such a good haul; the ship, its cargo, the men and a woman all at no cost of life or limb.

Rose felt the wave action shift as the boat veered and three men came to escort her above deck where she saw a small city, square ochre buildings piled upon each other with defensive walls humped above a port. The sun by now was blazing down and she felt herself breaking out into a sweat.

She was ushered down into a small boat and ferried to the wharf where she was placed on a mule-cart and taken up towards the citadel on the hill. There they pulled into a courtyard, aromatic with flowers and strange spicy smells. A man in flowing robes came out, eying her up and down. The men gestured to her to get out of the cart so that she could stand and the man could view her more fully.

As this was going on it seemed as if the leader and the man were arguing. Rose assumed with some sickness that they were arguing over the price to be paid for her, for every now and then the leader would gesture up and down her body as if praising her while the other would grunt, almost disparagingly. The other two men, the guards, looked on and it seemed as if they were suppressing lascivious giggles, "Like schoolboys," thought Rose.

Finally the man put his hand to his beard, grunted and seemed to say "Yes". At this he gestured to an assistant, who ran off to get some coins which were then handed over to the leader. He, feigning complaints, but secretly happy that his sales of contraband had begun so auspiciously, summoned the two guards and mounted the mule-cart back to the wharf, no doubt to sell the captain and crew into slavery and the ship and contents of the hold to the highest bidder.

No sooner had the corsairs left the courtyard than Rose was whisked off by several other women to the bath-house where they stripped her bare, washed her and applied fragrant oils. Rose felt a complex of emotions; fear for her future, anger at the intrusions into her privacy, pleasure at the bath and its fragrant emollients.

This done, she was lead to a cool airy room overlooking the courtyard, where it appeared that she, along with the several other women who were seated and reclining there, was supposed to wait until summoned.

"My God," thought Rose. "I must get out of here. I know what this man intends to do with me, what he already might be preparing to do."

"Don't fret yet, my dear," came the voice, startling Rose with its English intonation. "This man will leave you intact. He is just a go-between. It's your next owner you should worry about. You probably will sail tonight for Algiers. He'll get a better price for you there than in this backwater."

"What?" said Rose in astonishment.

"I know, my darling. Esther is the name," confided the young woman. "I was bound for Abidjan with my parents. They are both dead. We were taken off the coast of Mauretania. I was thirteen. The trader took a liking to me. Here I stay."

"But…" interceded Rose.

"Yes, I know. It seems unthinkable and of course it is. I am treated as if I were a possession of some sort. However, I find that at least I am a valued possession. I am fed, bathed and groomed, much like a lapdog. I am schooled and have many talents, but they are of no account here. Here, as I assure you, you will discover, one is, as a woman, a decoration, a symbol of a man's worth, a mule, or a dam—a producer of progeny. But I go on so. What is your story?"

"I am following my betrothed to Van Diemen's land…"

"Ah! In pursuit of love. A noble cause indeed. I was following my father and mother in their quest to bring light to the dark continent…and here I dwell, in this twilight state. I would wish you better fortune but it seems I am already too late."

"Is there really no hope?" asked Rose, thinking of her as yet undiscovered cache of money.

"Most unlikely, I fear. Being English, you have probably heard the saying, 'Do not try to rise above your station?'"

"Indeed. As a scullery maid, I heard it frequently from my master and my co-equals."

"A scullery maid!" exclaimed Esther, astonished at the incongruity of such a person, speaking in such a manner in such a place. "Well, here your station is approximately as I have described, and, just as in the "nook-shotten isle of Albion", you would do well to adjust to it."

"With respect Ma'am, that is such a dismaying thought, that I fear I must reject it. My love is, as we speak, being transported to the antipodes and I will find him."

"Well said. I wish you well."

Suddenly there was a noise at the door.

"I must not speak more," whispered Esther, grasping Rose's hand. "You sail tonight. Godspeed."

X

Evening fell to the sounds of chants from minarets all around. Soon after, a bevy of ladies came and prepared Rose for her journey. They bathed her yet again, rubbed her with sweet-smelling oils and finally wrapped in flowing silk robes, taking away her solid English clothes, gazing upon them and feeling them with some puzzlement. Rose could not help but be put in mind of how the pigs would be prepared for showing at the village fete back in Pyefleet. Despite her dire situation, she smiled at this.

As the dusk thickened she was lead down the stone staircase and out into the street where she was ushered onto a guarded carriage. In this, she rumbled down to the wharf where she was lead across a gangplank onto the sleek, lateen-sailed ship, much like the one of the corsairs that had abducted her.

Despite her best attempts at keeping her spirits enlivened, Rose felt herself slipping into a dizzying maelstrom of confusion and despair and was trying to compose herself when one of the ladies-in-waiting ran across the gangplank with her bag, containing sundries that were felt to be necessary for her trip. Upon receiving it, Rose stealthily felt it. The reassuring crumple of the banknotes helped still her nerves. There might still be hope.

In no time, they set sail, out of the harbor into the open sea for the trip around the bulge of North East Africa, through the straits of Gibraltar and on to the final destination, the place where she might spend the rest of her days, Algiers.

The ocean had a wide swell and a solid chop, but the boat cut through smoothly, much as she imagined the blades of the corsairs' scimitars would slice through flesh. The crew treated Rose very solicitously, most likely because she was a valuable cargo. Rose spent the night below deck, used by this time to the heaving and creaking of a ship. However, she was only able to sleep in small anxious bursts and would waken, become sorely aware of her plight and frenziedly think about what might befall her– as a slave, as a concubine, as a servant once more, forever separated from her Garrad, he who would live and die, never knowing of her pursuit of him, of how much she loved him.

Dawn broke sharply and quickly as the sun seemed to burst in a sparkling cascade across the waters. At the same instant, the captain and crew became very agitated, for they had seen something off the port bow. Rose steadied herself as she worked her way across the deck and gazed across the waves. No sooner did she see the ship that had occupied the crew's agitated attention than it issued two puffs of smoke. The crew ducked for cover, wailing, and then there was a twin whistling and screaming followed by two bursts of water, one short and one on the other side of the ship.

The entire crew seemed to cower. They looked to the captain for a decision as to whether they should fight, run or surrender. He issued a few brief commands and the crew set about obeying them. Rose was unsure as to which of the options the captain had decided upon until it seemed clear to her that the boat had stalled and the newly-sighted ship was approaching them at some speed.

Now that it seemed clear that the captain had decided not to lose his life, her attention fell onto the approaching gunboat. Was this yet another corsair? She thought not, for it was square rigged. After some minutes and intense squinting she made out the ship's name, "The Baltimore."

"American, perhaps," she thought. For she had heard how the United States had deployed marines in these waters to intercept and do battle with the Barbary Pirates. After a further interminable minute or two she could make out their blue uniforms, white pantaloons and saw the guns of all sorts trained on the now unfortunate corsairs, who seemed to be very careful not to appear hostile in any way, for the Baltimore was cocked and loaded.

Carefully and displaying great discipline, the Baltimore pulled alongside and the captain, accompanied by four men-at-arms, stepped aboard. The corsairs compliantly piled up their weapons on the deck and lined up with the newcomer's muskets and pistols trained upon them.

"Your ship is now under the command of the United States Marines. My name is Captain Isaac Ballenger and I am in command. Obey me and there will be no bloodshed. Brightman, take over this ship and prepare to sail for Gibraltar!"

Suddenly out of nowhere, one of the corsairs screamed, broke ranks and wielding a glinting sword, rushed at Ballenger, screaming. He advanced but a few paces when there was a loud crack issuing from the sails aloft in the marines' vessel. The man's chest reddened with a spot of blood as he stopped in his tracks and fell to deck, stone dead.

"Molloy, was that your handiwork?" cried out Captain Ballenger.

"Aye, Captain," came the reply from the sharpshooter high up in the rigging.

"You are shooting better, but next time try to catch him before he takes three steps towards me,"

"Aye, aye Captain," replied Molloy, smiling to himself in the furls of the rigging on high.

Ballenger smiled to himself and added, "Skipton, are you aloft and awake?"

"Aye, aye Captain," came the reply from high in the rigging.

"Skipton," enjoined the Captain, "I do hope our proceedings on board did not disrupt your slumbers."

"Aye, Captain, I mean no, Captain," came the somewhat mournful riposte from the marine ensconced in the furling sails above. It was the sound of a man who knew he was in trouble and was being toyed with.

"And you do understand that, as a sharpshooter, your task is to protect those on the boarding party and to occasionally let loose a volley?"

"Aye, aye, captain," replied Skipton sadly.

Ballenger shrugged and turned to the task at hand. "Put these men in irons and be ready to set sail," commanded Ballenger. At this, he finally noticed Rose.

"Madam, forgive me, I did not see you in all this commotion. I apologize for my rude introduction. I assume you are an enforced guest on this bark?"

"Indeed captain, I believe they were taking me to Algiers, for sale, no less. My name is Rose Flaxman. I am from Essex, England, on my way to meet my betrothed in Australia"

"Ah yes, of course. An interesting tale to be sure. My apologies, Madam, as you can see, I am currently quite occupied. We shall have a chance to become better

71

acquainted on our way to Gibraltar. Renwick, kindly escort this lady to quarters aboard our ship."

XI

"We are a young country," explained Ballenger as he turned his attention to Rose.

They were sitting at the captain's table eating fare that was finally somewhat familiar to her—boiled beef and cabbage. By now she had found her sea legs and was no longer afraid of sickness, so she ate heartily. In fact she had, at times, to restrain herself from gobbling down at a faster pace than the officers seated around the table.

"So I entreat you to forgive us our coarseness. Most of us are not ruffians, right, Spencer?" Spencer choked on his food and at this there was a gale of laughter around the table.

"I assure you, Captain, I find you not coarse at all, and after rescuing me, you would take on more the form of an angel," replied Rose and looking up, she saw the telltale sign in Ballenger's eyes that he was falling for her. She could not put her finger exactly on what it was, but it was as though a channel opened up between the surface of the man's eyes and his heart and then there was a certain deep softening. Sensing this, she stiffened and demurely returned to her plate. Ballenger may have sensed it also, for he turned the conversation.

"So you are in quest of your betrothed?"

"Indeed, sir. He was wrongly accused and sent to Van Diemen 's Land. I intend to find him."

"If he survives," blurted out one of the company and Ballenger shot him a steely gaze.

"I am, sure he will be fine, especially if he is sustained by the affections of one such as yourself madam," graciously interceded Ballenger.

Rose felt her eyes well up and her throat thicken. "Please excuse me. I must retire."

"Certainly madam. Finch, escort our guest to her quarters. We will be in Gibraltar by mid-morning."

XII

The stout, massive boulder that was Gibraltar gleamed in the morning sun as the Baltimore rhythmically rose and fell on the swell and finally reached the calm, seemingly still, waters of the port.

Ballenger escorted Rose to the Montserrat Hotel where she was pleased to hear the English intonation of the innkeeper. Finally, in her room, she was able, while absorbing the sounds and smells of the neighborhood wafting in through the sunny open window, to collect her thoughts and regain some order to her feelings.

"Dinner is being served on the terrace, madam," announced a voice from the other side of the door. Rose realized she was hungry and, after rinsing her face and hand in the bowl and pitcher, so like the ones at home in Essex, she ascended the stairs to the rooftop terrace, where she was greeted by a splendid glowing view of the rock, the harbor and the ocean beyond.

"Please, please join us!" came the request from a table in the shade. Rose looked and saw a young woman, with black, glowing eyes in a froth of lace, sitting next to a brown, middle-aged gentleman in an immaculate grey suit, gallantly cut and thinning sleeked back hair. They both smiled and Rose found herself curtseying and then joined them.

"Wonderful! Thank you for joining us. I am Evangelinha da Assis, and this is my companion and mentor, Mr. Chowdary. We are *en route* from Paris to Salvador, Brazil."

Rose smiled and nodded and Mr. Chowdary stood, bowed and said, "Enchanted!"

"I am Rose Flaxman, from Pyefleet, England, just rescued from the corsairs by a most gallant American marine. I am bound for Australia, in pursuit of my beloved."

"My goodness! So romantic! But then despite your much-vaunted starchiness, I find you English are quite a passionate people. Just look at your poetry, your literature. I wish you good luck in your quest," said Evangelinha, her English immaculate with but a slight accent.

"And you shall find him, madame, for you two must be from the same soul, you must have many karmas over one another," opined Mr. Chowdary, the words seeming to come from out of nowhere.

Rose must have looked puzzled for Evangelinha interjected quickly, "Mr. Chowdary is a philosopher, a wise man and he sees into things deeply. We met in Paris, while I was studying at the Sorbonne and he has arranged to teach in Salvador. But surely, you will accompany us? Our ship leaves for Salvador in two days as it is being re-fitted here. I insist upon it. We make such an interesting trio."

At this, the meal was served. Mr. Chowdary eating only vegetables, looked up at Rose as he felt her observing him. He smiled and nodded at her, reassuringly. Rose felt strangely calmed by his gestures of prescience.

Evangelinha must have noticed this exchange, for she remarked, "Mr. Chowdary believes in karma. It is a most subtle and enchanting philosophy. We have many lifetimes and when we die we are reborn into a new life where we inherit the debts and assets acquired in our previous lifetimes. The aim, as I understand it, is to reduce both of those to zero. Thus we are no longer held bound to this sorry place by the necessity to make good on our debts or liquidate our assets. Have I learned well, Mr. Chowdary?"

"Indeed you have," he replied, "I would but add that we, at this very table, must have all met before. We must find out how we are entangled in the infinite web of karma."

Rose and Evangelinha glanced at each other and smiled.

XIII

Breakfast on the terrace the following morning was a sparkling affair with the sun glinting on the distant ocean, the tinkling of china, sea-bells and cutlery all around. Despite her longing and the gaping hole she experienced at missing her beloved, Rose felt a pang of intense joy.

"We are of the same size, I believe," said Evangelinha. "I have many trunks of clothes purchased in Paris. After breakfast, you must feel free to select," she added with something of a mischievous sparkle to her dark eyes. Rose was very grateful, for she was still wearing the flowing robes with which she had been adorned by her erstwhile captors.

Mr. Chowdary smiled and said, "Let us take a moment to give thanks to the Great Creator for endowing us with a human life."

"Indeed," replied Evangelinha, "And we must also give thanks that Rose was delivered from captivity."

"Our paths have crossed before. We must pay close attention to how our karmas play out."

"Well one way involves us securing Rose passage with us on our ship."

Breakfast was served. Amongst the fare were some kippers. Rose ate them with relish while the others looked on, puzzled, bemused by such strange breakfast fare.

When breakfast was finished, a waiter handed Rose a card, saying that a gentleman was waiting for her in the lounge. Puzzled, she excused herself and went downstairs. In the lounge she saw Captain Ballenger cutting the finest of figures in his blue and white uniform.

"I do not wish to importune you ma'am, and I apologize for the early hour. We sail at noon. I simply wish to reassure myself as to your well-being," he offered, stiffly.

Rose smiled to herself, sensing his anxiety at this new context, these feelings he seemed to have for her, and said, "Why, you bother me not one whit, sir. You are most kind, most gallant."

"My thanks. I trust you are recovered from your ordeal?"

"Indeed, captain, and again I must express my deepest gratitude to you and your men for my rescue, words cannot...." And at this she found herself welling up with an unanticipated emotion. Her eyes moistened and her throat thickened. Ballenger, ruffled in his pockets, found a handkerchief and offered it. She demurred, regaining her composure.

"The pleasure was all mine. I am glad to be of service. I shall be here in these waters some while, I think. But I, without doubt, will be returning to Norfolk, Virginia where I reside. The address is on the card delivered to you. I am not sure how to say this, but I must…Miss Flaxman, if for any reason, you should find yourself disposed to visit the United States, it would be more than an honor, it would be…"

Rose interrupted him, recognizing immediately that the only way this could happen would be if she failed to reunite with Garrad, an eventuality she refused to countenance. "Why thank you kind sir, you are indeed gracious. If I am there, I shall be sure to visit you. How could I not?" By this she intended not to get his hopes up. She noted to herself that the intuition she had had at dinner on board ship had been correct.

"My thanks. I wish you the very best in your quest, and of course," he added discreetly, "the invitation stands for you and your betrothed."

"Again, one thousand thanks."

They lapsed into an uncomfortable silence for some seconds, at the same time becoming aware that they were the object of some interest to other denizens of the lounge. The heat was also starting to build in the room as the sun climbed in the sky outside.

"Well, I must set sail," said Ballenger. "Bon voyage. I wish you all the best of good fortune in your quest. He is indeed a lucky man to have one so devoted as you in search of him," and he swallowed and attempted to steel his eyes, bowed ever-so-slightly and turned and left as Rose said, "Thank-you…thank…"

XIV

"Soon we shall cross the equator," said Mr. Chowdary to Rose as they, accompanied by Evangelinha, gazed at the clear night sky over the stern of the Mae de Santos, the ship that had borne them out from Gibraltar and was scudding southwards towards Salvador, Brazil.

"You will like Salvador," added Evangelinha, "It is a very mystical place, very spiritual. Soon, we shall see the stars of the southern cross."

"Ah, the stars," intervened Mr. Chowdary, "There is the North Star, that is the saint," he added, with an attitude that indicated he wanted a question. He had something to teach.

"A saint?" asked Rose.

"Ah yes, Miss Flaxman. Long ago, there was a saint and he told God that he wanted to be a guide for humans for all time, so that they would not lose their way. God granted his wish and let him become the North Star."

"My goodness! What strange and lovely stories you tell, Mr. Chowdary," said Evangelinha after the import of the tale and sunk in.

"Yes, indeed," said Mr. Chowdary. "This story tells us many things, all at once. Most importantly, I believe, it tells us about love, how love can guide the way. Do you not agree, Miss Flaxman?"

Rose was quite shaken by the sudden turn of the conversation toward her and felt emotion welling up from deep inside. However, when Evangelinha placed a consoling hand on her arm, she was able to respond.

"Quite, Mr. Chowdary. I agree entirely," she replied.

They continued in silence, listening to the skimming of the waves as the ship made good headway, feeling something of a chill as they countenanced the spangled blue-black sky. Every now and then they caught a glimpse, in the shadows above, the darker, angular, arched wings of the Frigate Birds, forever following, effortlessly hovering, gliding.

Chapter 4

I

A stiff steady breeze ruffled the grey waters of the Pyefleet channel as Kitty made her way along the sea wall to see Mrs. Moffett. It had been a week since Rose's departure and all were concerned as to her whereabouts, especially Mrs. Moffett, who loved her so dearly and had taken her under her wing. Kitty had two intentions in mind, first, to comfort Mrs. Moffett and secondly to enlist her help.

"Oh, Kitty, my dear. My godfather's, it's been such a while and what with all that's been going on. Sit down my dear, I shall make you a nice cuppa tea," exclaimed Mrs. Moffett, exuberantly warm, as always.

"Thank you Mrs. Moffett. That would be lovely. I came to reassure you as to Rose's wellbeing. I fear I cannot tell you exactly where she is or what she is doing, since I am sworn to secrecy, but I can tell you she is well cared for and is doing that which she feels compelled to do."

"It's about that terrible affair with Garrad, I'll wager," replied Mrs. Moffett as she put the kettle on the stove.

Kitty nodded subtly but said, "I can say no more."

"I understand my dear. Just so long as I know she has come to no harm—it would be like Rose to be headed for Van Diemen's land, after Garrad…" added Mrs. Moffett.

The look on Kitty's face betrayed that Mrs. Moffett had stumbled upon the truth and it stopped them both in their tracks.

"Oh my goodness! But how?" exclaimed Mrs. Moffett in a whisper.

"Not a word to anyone."

"I understand Miss. I am sorry for having…it was quite unintentional like.."

"It is nothing. I am sure I can trust you. Besides, I do have another issue, I would like to discuss with you."

"Go ahead, my dear."

"I hate to incommode you, or put you in an uncomfortable position, or in any way imply…"

"Oh out with it my precious, we are all family!" encouraged Mrs. Moffett.

"Very well. Rumor has it that you are acquainted with Toby Pegg, and that he, by virtue of the fact that he is often being pursued by coastguards and revenue men is very knowledgeable of the comings and goings in these waters."

"Indeed. He is."

"So I was wondering if he might be willing to tell you of the arrival of any boats or ships carrying Frenchmen up the channels for purposes of spying."

"Lawks! What! Boney's men around here, spying. Why…"

"Yes, Mrs. Moffett. It is very serious. Just before Garrad was falsely accused and transported, he and Rose heard some people, under cover of darkness," and here Kitty rolled her eyes and pointed upstairs so as to indicate she meant in the immediate neighborhood, "speaking in French with a visiting stranger. She mentioned it once on a visit and it excited my father's suspicions which he shared with me"

"And I should ask Toby if he knows of these visitors?" asked Mrs. Moffett, as if everything was falling into place for her.

"Could you?"

"But why?" asked Mrs. Moffett, indicating with a roll of her eyes the house where the master and mistress lived, not wanting to utter the dangerous, deadly implications out loud.

"Who knows? Debts, blackmail, money—any of these could overcome the love of one's country in a weak person."

"I s'll ask Toby tonight. He'll be at his regular haunt, The Peldon Rose."

"Thank you Mrs. Moffett. Be sure to ask if he has noticed any regular schedule of these visitations, if they occur at all."

"I shall, miss. And we shall get to the bottom of this. Visits by Boney's men, gives me the very shivers."

II

Mrs. Moffett entered the Peldon Rose public house which was thick with smoke and din. Two old chaps were demonstrating a morris dance step with fluttering handkerchiefs. She squirmed by and saw old Toby, clay pipe in hand, by the fireplace, in his usual spot. As she approached he saw her and exclaimed, "Why, it's my old darlin' Meg!" and he scooted over to make space for her next to the fireplace. "Sue!" he called out to the serving-girl, "Two more mulled ales my darling, if you please." Sue nodded and squeezed through to the bar.

"Well we don't see much of you these days my dear, since you've been up at the house," commenced Toby. "I trust you are well?"

"I am Toby, but you are right on all counts. They are keeping me so busy up there I scarcely have time to breathe. But I am not here only for the stolen pleasure of your company."

Toby laughed at this. "Well what is it that brings you here, my pigeon?"

"Well," she replied, lowering her voice and leaning towards Toby, "We, that is, Kitty Highweather and myself, have reason to believe that some French have been visiting these waters to carry out some spying. And we was wondering, since you are the most familiar with every twist and turn, if you might have seen anything."

Toby was blindsided by this and he paused as he glanced around the bar to ensure no eyes were upon them. "Well, I have heard some fools blundering about every so often. Like as not they don't know where they're goin'—last time was a few weeks back, afore young Garrad got sent off. I didn't hear 'em speak or see their boat, maybe a skiff, as the tide was runnin' fast. It was up by Beggar's Creek, just off the Pyefleet."

"Beggars Creek, so up towards the house?" asked Mrs. Moffett, her face and voice thickening with suspicion.

Toby picked up on her intimations. "I didn't want to say anything for fear of drawing attention. Revenuers you know. French, you say? Spying on us?"

"And maybe talking to some locals," added Mrs. Moffett. "So the next time…"

"Next time I'll have Jim Varley signal from over at St. Osyth and he can tell constable there's something strange in Beggar's Creek" offered Toby.

"Thank you Toby. I know you want to stay clear of trouble and this puts you somewhat in the light. I think we might need more than old constable Pike to deal with this matter, but that could be the start."

"Tis alright my dear. I hate revenuers but I will not have Boney and his like in my waters. Ah, here is our ale! Heat up the poker my dear."

And Mrs. Moffett heated the poker and sizzled it into the ales, being careful not to touch the sides of the glass. Together they supped deeply at the warm, smoky, hearty brew.

III

A fine grey mist was rolling in off the North Sea. At intervals, a small breeze might catch the grey miasma and swirl it into small vortices that twisted and turned across the marshes. The mist coalesced into droplets on the sedges, gorse and broom bushes. Mrs. Moffett was in the heat of her kitchen, busily ordering the scullery maid as she prepared lunch for those in the dining room above.

Frederick, the stable boy, was eating his lunch, a pork pie, and quaffing a pitcher of ale by the window. As he looked up he saw a form approaching in the distance along the sea wall, now enveloped, now emerging from the banks of mist.

"Someone approaching," he called out to the company in the kitchen.

"Who? The parson? Another one for lunch?"

"Don't know," replied Frederick. "Big coat, big hat, looks well off."

"Now you have sparked my curiosity," said Mrs. Moffett as she wiped her hands on her pinafore and stepped over to the window. Squinting, and adjusting her gaze to allow for the distortions in the glass she peered and peered. "I have no idea who that might be. Well they must be coming here, and they certainly look determined. We shall find out soon. Keep looking young sir Frederick. I must be about my business." She returned to the cooking pots and Frederick continued to look but he said nothing except, "I don't know who it is."

After several long minutes, Frederick announced, with some alarm, "He's coming up the back path! He's coming to the kitchen."

"Well we will just have to tell him of his error and send him to the main door," admonished Mrs. Moffet.

No sooner had she said this than a tall, dark figure of a man was standing in the doorway of the kitchen. He was wearing a thick, finely embroidered coat and shoes that were meant for the paved streets of the city, smeared with the mud of the sea wall path. He was around fifty years of age and had a dark well-trimmed beard that only partially concealed the deep creases in his well-worn face. His eyes glowed with a deep, heart-felt warmth and were deep black-brown, almost like the gypsies of the nearby woods. Mrs. Moffett was struck by his handsome demeanor. He doffed his hat, and said, "I beg your pardon for arriving unannounced and at what seems to be a busy time. Do I speak with Mrs. Moffett?"

Taken aback by having her name known to a complete stranger, she replied, "Why yes sir, may I be so bold as to inquire…"

"Yes of course. I will get straight to the point. My name is Benjamin Flaxman. I am the father of Rose Flaxman."

Mrs. Moffett nearly fainted. The two scullery maids, Molly and Jenny, and Frederick simply gaped and stared.

Flaxman filled in the silence. "I know. You thought me lost to the gin-alleys of London. So did I. But I am reformed. I know I have done wrong and I intend to mend that which I have broken."

"Ah yes! As I look at you now I can see you are indeed Rose's long-departed father. Molly, Jenny, Frederick, please be about your business. Mr. Flaxman and I must talk." When Mrs. Moffett was sure they were out of earshot, she continued, "You look as though you have seen many woes, if I may be so bold. But sir, Ben", remonstrated Mrs. Moffett, "She has been gone over a month now. Gone for Australia…"

"I know. Her beloved was falsely accused, or so I am told by the people I have spoken to in the village. I have three goals. One, to see justice done. Two, to reunite with my dear daughter whom I have so deeply wronged, and three, to do all I can to bring about her lasting happiness."

"Well, you are certainly not alone in having those aims and purposes," replied Mrs. Moffett. Then, suddenly catching the situation, she said, "Please, sit down, here by the stove. Warm your bones. Would you like some ale?" At this Flaxman raised his hand in gentle protest. "No drink, sir? How about a nice cup of tea? And soon I'll have some cottage pie ready."

"That sounds most excellent," said Flaxman, as he took a seat by the stove, rubbing his hands together.

"I feel I must tell you my story, if I may," said Flaxman.

"I'm all ears my dear," encouraged Mrs. Moffett, already feeling the familiarity with the Ben Flaxman of years ago returning.

"As you can remember, I was very distraught by the passing of my wife. I was not strong. It was like a great black pit opened up inside of me and I fell into it. Soon I fell to drinking and bad ways and found myself in "Gin Lane" as they call it. Somewhere in London. I know not where. I couldn't take you there today. And so I languished in an ever deepening pit of depravity. I cannot describe the coarseness of my ways for fear of offending you or any good company."

"Oh, I am sure we have heard it all here," interrupted Mrs. Moffett, "and besides, we are taught not to judge. I am sorry, go on."

"Well," continued Ben, "so my ways continued and I am certain I should have met with an early death were it not for the kind intervention of a saint, although he recoils at such a nomination, a Mr. Ernest Glastonbury. I was laying on some steps, almost unconscious from overconsumption of gin when this gentleman, God alone knows why, stoops over me and asks if I needed help. Even though I had long since given up on life and was but hoping for a peaceful painless death, I somehow had the wherewithal to say yes and so he helped me up and escorted me to a meeting house. And there I lodged for several weeks, sobering up. I soon discovered that

Mr. Glastonbury was an active member of a group, perhaps you have heard of them, The Society of Friends?"

"Indeed I have, Ben. There is such a meeting house in Colchester," interjected Mrs. Moffett.

"So I became part of their society, regularly attending meetings. We would sit and speak freely as we felt the impulse so to do, always trying to become a closer friend of Jesus."

"My godfather's!" exclaimed Mrs. Moffett.

"I know," responded Ben. "At first I thought it strange. There was no leader, no minister, everyone an equal, as we are in the eyes of the Lord, I suppose. Anyway, as time passed and I became more sober, more right in my head, Mr. Glastonbury introduced me to some of his colleagues and I learned the businesses they were in– things like banking, buttons, clothing, shoes, chocolate, all sorts of enterprises and very successful too. Slowly but surely I made my way and made a successful living."

"Goodness, what a tale."

"But for the longest time I could not do what I knew what was right, to correct the wrong I had done in leaving my poor little Rose, all alone, motherless, and then without a father. I felt so guilty and ashamed."

"Oh my goodness," said Mrs. Moffett, searching within herself for words that might comfort this man in his deep distress.

Ben Flaxman nodded as if he could appreciate her difficulty in coming up with words to match his deep pain. "But eventually I saw that my shame and guilt were just selfish indulgences. In addition, I have now enough money to make some gesture of amends to the little girl, of course, she is now grown, whom I have wronged so."

"And now, she is gone off to goodness knows where," added Mrs. Moffett.

"Yes," assented Ben, "and you might imagine the anguish I felt when I first heard this in my inquiries in town and of course from Parson Highweather and Kitty. Nevertheless, I shall find her and these wrongs shall be righted."

"Well, plans are already afoot in that regard," replied Mrs. Moffett, cautiously. "Molly, Jenny! Come in here and take the food and drink upstairs. Frederick, go see to the stable, my boy! I think I hear the horses getting restive." They duly and briskly obeyed.

When Mrs. Moffett was certain they were gone, she stepped closer to Ben and lowered her voice. "We, that is, Miss Kitty, the parson's daughter and I, believe, along with almost all around here, that it was Sir Sydney and Squire Paxton conspired to have Garrad sent away. We further are of the opinion that they and Lady Charlotte have been meeting someone who speaks French, if you catch my drift."

Taken aback, and sharply sucking air through his teeth, Ben Flaxman replied, "I think I do catch your drift, Mrs. Moffett, but what can we do?"

"Miss Kitty and I are going to London this coming Friday. We are going to Admiralty House or some-such. We plan to arouse suspicion amongst the proper quarters and catch them."

"I shall come with you," interjected Ben without a moment's hesitation.

"Oh would you sir? It would help to have a man of such standing and, dare I say, connections, speak on our behalf," said Mrs. Moffett with considerable relief, for this task had been weighing on her.

"I would. I am torn, for I want to be reunited as soon as possible but to set off knowing that those who have wronged my long-lost child have had their just desserts dished out to them would comfort my soul enormously," said Ben.

"I understand, sir," replied Mrs. Moffett. "Let us pray that we may resolve this with haste. You might recall Toby?"

"Yes."

"Well he is the only other one as knows and he is keeping a close eye on things in the channel. Also Jim Varley in Saint Osyth is keeping watch. With luck, they shall be caught before the month is out, and you can be on your way to find your, I should say, our, dear Rose."

"Friday you say?"

"Yes we shall take the coach from the Peldon Rose to Heybridge that leaves at six. It's my day off. Not a word to anyone."

"I understand Mrs. Moffett. I am staying at the Peldon Rose, so it will be but a few steps to the coach. I think I will go before I am noticed."

"Godspeed, sir," said Mrs. Moffett as she saw him to the door.

Ben Flaxman stepped out and walked towards the long, curving sea wall. The mist had lifted and the sun was straining through a thin high layer of milky clouds. His step seemed somewhat lighter and even more determined than before.

IV

The morning was crisp as Kitty, Mrs. Moffett and Ben Flaxman mounted the carriage bound for Heybridge, where they would take a connection to London where they would seek an audience with someone in Admiralty. Kitty imagined that since the business was being conducted by sea and up the channels of the marshes near her home that the navy would be interested.

The morning was crisp, as some grey cumulus mustered in the west, but the road was dry and not too rutted. They made good time, in relative silence and made good their connection to London, arriving in the late evening. Benjamin had them take a hansom cab to his home in Pimlico.

"From here, we are but a stone's throw from the people we will need to talk to. I am certain they will be most interested in what you might have to share," said Ben, catching the two ladies attention for but a moment as they stared through the cab's windows.

They arrived at Flaxman's house shortly. It was a fine house but, as might be expected from his history, not pretentious or needlessly ostentatious.

"My, sir! Such a nice abode, and so convenient to everything," complimented Mrs. Moffett.

"Thank you," replied Ben, adding as they climbed the steps to the oaken door, "Mrs. Crispin will see too it you are comfortably situated and she will bring you some viands and cheese. I suggest we start our quest at nine o' clock tomorrow, if you are agreeable?"

"Yes, indeed sir, of course," said Mrs. Moffett.

"Indeed," replied Kitty.

"Kitty," said Ben, in a somewhat throaty voice, "Words cannot express how happy I am to be in your acquaintance. I know you have been as a sister to my precious, long-lost daughter. I know that this must have brought her great pleasure and comfort through all her travails. For this I will be everlastingly grateful."

Kitty, unused to such a direct expression of thoughts and emotion, was at a temporary loss for words. She was also aware that she would have to share with Ben Flaxman the true destination of his daughter. She also felt that he, sensing her closeness to Rose, perhaps had suspicions that she knew of her whereabouts. Finally she managed, "I am sure, sir, I am the fortunate one. I miss her dearly, but the times I spent with her were the best of my life."

"And as to her whereabouts?" inquired Flaxman, sensing Kitty was holding back something.

"In quest of Garrad in Van Diemen's land," she replied.

Flaxman gasped, shook his head as if he had been hit and then smiled. "She has a strong spirit, like her mother. Thank you, Kitty, when this business is settled, I will find her."

At this all retired.

V

The three stepped out of the sharp, bright sun into the dusky, oak-lined corridors of the Admiralty.

"We are in luck," muttered Flaxman, "through my dealings I know some of these people."

"Goodness," replied Mrs. Moffett as both she and Kitty were taking in the resplendent architecture of the place.

"I should like to see Rear Admiral Farnborough. You may tell him it is Ben Flaxman," he said to a quill-bearing clerk sitting at a prominently placed desk, in effect, standing guard to the interior offices. The man hesitated, beckoned to a messenger nearby and whispered in his ear. The messenger set off briskly.

A few minutes later, the messenger returned and the secretary gestured that the three could follow him, which they did. They followed down a large corridor and were finally ushered through a huge oak door where a grey-whiskered, aging man greeted them heartily.

"Ben, old chap! So good to see you, and with two beautiful English roses, if I may be so bold! What brings you here? Not bad news, I hope? Excuse me. I forget myself. Please be seated, make yourself comfortable. Here, may I suggest the sofa, ladies. A wooden chair for you, Ben, eh!" joked Farnborough. Ben smiled at this allusion to his religious practices.

"Anyway. To what do I owe the pleasure?" asked Farnborough.

As Kitty and Mrs. Moffett unfolded their story, with an occasional explanatory interjection from Ben, Farnborough's mood changed from one of hearty bonhomie to one of serious concern. He sat behind his desk, asking clarifying questions and taking notes as he shifted from old friend, hail-fellow-well-met, to his official role as one charged with protecting the nation.

Finally, he sucked in a deep breath, raised his eyebrows and said, "You know, I know these chaps?"

"Who?" they all three asked at once.

"Sir Sydney and Squire Paxton. I used to belong to the same club. None of this must go beyond these walls, you understand? Don't go there any more. Rum chaps. Big gamblers. Opium even. Always shady coves looking for them at the door. Plus they were involved in activities I do not feel free to enumerate in the presence of ladies," said Farnborough, almost ruminating to himself, pondering his options.

Finally, it was as if he had decided. "These are dangerous times," he exclaimed. "We must pursue everything, for they would chop off the head of our dear king. I am sorry to discomfit you ladies," he quickly added. He rang a bell and instantly the messenger who had escorted them to the office entered.

"Fetch me Mr. Blakesley if you please," commanded Farnborough.

"Yes sir, at once sir."

Within a minute of tense waiting Mr. Blakesley entered, tall, dashing and mustachioed.

"Mr. Blakesley, I have an assignment for you. You are to wear civilian clothing. Accompany these ladies to their home in Pyefleet. I assume there is an inn there?" he inquired of Flaxman.

"Indeed sir, I stay there myself."

"Stay at that inn. Reveal to no-one your true identity and purpose. Speak to these ladies and this gentleman. Take good note of what they tell you. Collaborate with their friends at Pyefleet. I believe we are to catch some French spies."

"Very good sir," replied Blakesley, glancing at Mrs. Moffett, Flaxman and Kitty. As he looked at Kitty his heart skipped several beats and he felt momentarily dizzy. Finally, he regained his senses.

"Well I think we are done here. I have reports to make. You have spies to catch. I bid you Godspeed," said Farnborough, already looking at the papers on his desk. "Adieu, ladies and to you my Flaxman, my dear friend, good luck in your quest."

Once outside, the four, Blakesley, Flaxman, Mrs. Moffett and Kitty, gathered together under one of the fine old mottled plane trees lining the avenue.

It was as if Flaxman had been planning all along, so clear were his ideas. "We still have time for the coach back to Pyefleet. There we shall meet with Toby and, what was his name?"

"Jim Varley," replied Mrs. Moffett.

"Yes, Varley. And we shall fashion a plan to trap these scoundrels and set right some wrongs. Adjutant Blakesley, you will need time to prepare, no doubt, but perhaps you can catch the coach tomorrow. I trust you have an extra pistol or two?'

"Indeed Mr. Flaxman. I will come fully equipped," he replied.

"Goodness me! Pistols!" exclaimed Mrs. Moffett. Kitty blanched. Blakesley gestured towards her and hesitated.

"No fear, Mrs. Moffett," said Flaxman. "I learned a thing or two during my days in the gin alleys, amongst many wily coves and I am certain Mr. Blakesley here is fully competent."

"Is there a good constable at Pyefleet?" inquired Blakesley of Kitty.

"There is, a Mr. Pike. A stout fellow in every sense of the word. Not too fast on his feet, I'm afraid."

"Good," replied Blakeslee, "I think we shall fashion a plan in which Varley and Toby, Pegg, is it? will tell of the whereabouts of the miscreants and Mr. Flaxman and I shall apprehend them, for I assume you wish to take part in this venture, sir?"

"Of course," swiftly responded Flaxman.

"Good. And then we shall hand them over to Constable Pike."

"Perhaps more easily said than done," ventured Kitty.

"Precisely," agreed Blakeslee, "But time presses. I bid you goodbye and look forward to seeing you again in Pyefleet, where, of course, we must be as strangers so as not to stimulate curiosity. Ladies," said Blakesley as he bowed. He shook hands with Flaxman and briskly turned on his heel and marched back into the Admiralty.

Chapter 5

I

"Van Diemen's land my donkeys!" yelled the mate down through the hatch, careful not to breathe the foul stench of vomit, rotting food and faeces. Two swabs were sent below to roust Garrad and his sad fellows from their stupor and they were led, almost dragged, on deck. There, in the misty distance, they saw the green limned hills and shoreline of what was to be their home. On the left, waves broke on blackened rocks as they hove into the makeshift harbor.

On the jetty they were greeted by their overseers who desultorily pointed out the men they would take in their service. Garrad was selected by a burly, bearded plug of a man called Makepeace who duly led him up the muddy slope between the shacks and into the forest behind the settlement. There, in the shade of the deep green overhanging trees, they came upon a hut with smoke issuing from a tin-pipe chimney.

Makepeace broke his silence with, "I'll feed you today, but that's it. From tomorrow you feed yourself. We're on rations here. You may join the others on the shoreline and gather seaweed, crabs, limpets, whatever you find." Garrad was exhausted and felt dizzy. He did not reply.

"Follow," ordered Makepeace gruffly. "I'll show you your crib," and he led Garrad round the back of his hut to where there was a lean-to of old ship boards and brushwood.

"I'll let you rest for an hour or so. Then you must pull my plough."

Garrad crawled into the nest of straw under the planks and curled up, hoping for the oblivion of sleep.

II

Garrad slept fitfully, pestered by insects and still feeling the rock of the boat, even though he was on dry land. Makepeace prodded him with a stick to wake him after what seemed like a few minutes. Garrad felt as though his veins were filled not with blood, but with brine and he almost fainted as he stood up.

"Here. This shall be your harness," said Makepeace as he handed Garrad a tangle of old coarse rope. Garrad looked at it befuddled. "Look lively man! You wear it like this," and Makepeace forced the rope harness over Garrad's head and around his chest. "I need to get an acre ploughed before sundown. You may eat afterwards."

Makepeace led Garrad out through the trees where there was a sort of clearing, strewn with boulders and tree stumps. A crude plough stood at the base of a tree and Makepeace readied it and Garrad to be hitched.

"Alright, now pull when I say pull and stop when I say stop. No slacking, or I shall resort to this," and he tapped the whip he had in his belt by his side. "And remember," he added, "If that's not enough, there always further transportation to Norfolk Island. This is paradise compared to that, so watch your step my lad."

The sun had risen and the clearing was as hot as a furnace. Soon Garrad felt himself losing his grip on his sanity as Makepeace's commands rang out, "Pull! Pull! Stop! Stop!" At almost every step there was a rock or a root to be pried loose and the soil was thick and shiny clay. Garrad slipped and fell every yard or so and Makepeace cursed him. His lips were cracked and he was parched. The ropes ate into his flesh and chafed until his shoulders were a mess of blood and clay. Finally Garrad collapsed into the mud and, try as he might he could not stir. Even a couple of lashes from Makepeace's whip made no impression. Finally Makepeace sat down under a bush and lit his pipe. He looked up at the sun which was edging below the tree-tops and said, "Alright. That is a start, but I shall endure no more slacking. I am serious about Norfolk. Ask the others. Now take off the harness, pick up those logs and carry them back to the cabin."

Back at the shack, Makepeace lit a fire and reheated some greasy slop with some fatty gobbets of meat and, breaking off a hunk of bread, passed it to Garrad who despite its unfathomably disgusting nature, gorged it, feeling its energy suffusing his entire body.

"It's late. We shall start early tomorrow. That's the last meal I'll provide. Now, go to your shelter and sleep and, by the way, you are welcome to attempt an escape. Those forests, mountains and that ocean are filled with dead men who will tell you the tale of their misadventure," and he laughed at his bitter witticism.

Garrad was beyond caring and sagged off to the lean-to. He fell asleep swiftly, but his slumber was disrupted several times by terrifying sharp screams issuing from the forest around, some sharp yelps of pain, some long despairing groans, some were yells from other men telling everyone to shut up. Garrad thought to himself that he must have entered yet another circle of hell.

III

Garrad was finally awoken in the grim half-light of dawn. It was freezing and all around there was a cacophony of strange bird calls, even of beasts as the surrounding forest awoke.

"We must go down to the shore. Food," announced Makepeace.

Garrad's body was stiff from months of not moving and then the exertions of yesterday as he hobbled and limped down the narrow, rock-strewn pathway. Finally he could smell the tang of salt water and seaweed. Then he heard the soughing of waves. Then the trees gave way to a small meadow. Beyond was an acre or so of boulders. Beyond that, the sea.

"There is your breakfast," said Makepeace, again seeming to enjoy his dark humour as he gestured to the rocks.

Garrad was puzzled, but as he looked at the rocks, the truth became clear as he saw, with a sinking heart, that there were several men scavenging among the rock pools. Some were scraping off seaweed, others looking for something under boulders that they turned over. Others were bearing pointed sticks and spearing into the rock pools. He was to gather his meal from this grey-green shoreline.

"Yes. The supply ships are a little slow in arriving," said Makepeace. "Get to it, Essex boy! We haven't got all day!"

Garrad hobbled and scrambled over the rocks, slipping several times on the green slimy weed, completely at a loss as to what was edible, knowing that he must eat something or his wasted body would collapse forever.

"The limpets are best, but you'll have to venture a little further," came a ringing voice that astonished Garrad in its upper class nasal clarity and intonation. He turned and saw a tall, scrawny, straggle-haired man several yards away with a rounded cobble in his hand. "You will need one of these and a stout stick to knock them off. Here, I have a spare." And the man tossed Garrad a stick. "Look around for a good stone."

Garrad picked up the stick and found a round stone. Then he must have looked bewildered. "Ah yes, of course! No limpets where you come from? I'll wager. I'm from Cornwall, plenty there. Banks is the name, but they call me Colonel. A limpet is the little blackish-brownish, cone shaped thing adhering to these rocks. Doesn't want to let go, needs a good belt and then inside a salty morsel. Keeps you going. Here, I'll show you."

"Come on! Get a move on!" yelled Makepeace from the shore where he was sitting on a log, munching on a chunk of bread. "Food, not conversation!"

Banks came over to where Garrad was standing. "Look! Here's one. Bash it like this," and he positioned the stick next to the lip of the limpet, "and belt it, so!" and he thumped the stone against the stick. The limpet squished loose and Banks offered it to Garrad who pried the wet nugget of salty, slimy meat from the shell, grateful, for all that, for some nourishment. "If you are quick, and you supplement with some stalks of this," at which he gestured to some green stalks sprouting in the shallows of a rock pool, "you'll make it through the day. Do not be finicky," he admonished.

Garrad set about harvesting his breakfast, prying limpets from the rocks and eating the salty stalks of seaweed. Slowly but surely he felt the nourishment enter his body. He still was hungry, however, when Makepeace and the other overseers gathered on the shoreline yelled out for them to return.

Working their way back to the shore across the rocks, he was joined by Banks.

"Thanks for your help," said Garrad

"You are welcome, old chap, or should I say, mate? Your crime?"

"None. They say I poached."

"Ah! Mine, my old mate, was challenging the wrong person to a duel, wounding him and then discovering that he was very good friends with a magistrate who, shall we say, owed him a favour? I was found guilty of attempted murder. Given my service to the country and my standing, they were kind enough not to hang me but to send me here."

All Garrad could do was shake his head and blow a sharp puff of air in response to this story. They were nearing the overseers.

Makepeace called out, "Time for work my salts! Conversation time is over."

Banks' overseer, a crooked, haggard man in rags yelled out, "Come on Colonel! Time for your drill!"

Before Banks stepped away towards his overseer, he muttered to Garrad, "We must escape while we still have strength."

IV

Garrad's shoulders became infected from the constant chafing of the plough harness he was forced to pull every day, Makepeace threatening the whip or transportation to Norfolk Island, where conditions were far worse. Each morning he was lead down to the shoreline, accompanied by Makepeace's scrawny dogs, to collect his daily victuals and each day he could feel his strength ebbing. One morning Banks, came across a birds nest with four eggs. He called Garrad over to the spot and gave him two of them. They were buff-coloured and brown streaked, still warm from the bird that had been sitting on them.

"Swallow it whole, without asking any questions or letting it stay in your mouth, else you will puke," advised Colonel Banks. He demonstrated the technique, downing each egg in one swift movement so as not to witness its contents in his mouth and throat. Garrad hesitated, but Banks insisted, "Quick, before anyone else sees us. You need this strength." Garrad swallowed the crunchy, glutinous, cartilaginous slime in as close to one gulp as he could manage. Then he concentrated on not vomiting and swallowed the next. It was as if he could feel the strength from the eggs feeding immediately into his body and he nodded to Banks.

"We must be strong for our escape," whispered Banks. "I have been constructing a raft. In a week or so we will drag it down to the Derwent River, float out to sea and sail free. We will hug the coastline around to the north of the island and then we shall find a good spot, build a better boat and head over the Bass Strait to Australia, where we shall find a spot to live out our lives as free men."

"What are you two up to over there? No talking you dogs! Garrad Hansen, my ploughshare! Get back over here! You have some heaving to do."

"Go," muttered Banks. "In a week or two my raft will be seaworthy."

V

It was damp and chilly and Garrad reckoned that it must be about two in the morning as he crept out of his shelter. He had been doing his best to train Makepeace's dogs to just greet him with snuffling rather than barking and fortunately they only sniffed him and then curled up back to sleep. Garrad moved excruciatingly slowly for fear of waking Makepeace until he was sure he was out of earshot. Then he struck out quickly through the forest, up to the ridge crest and then down into the next valley. The going was wet underfoot and he slipped several times. Already he could feel the deep fatigue in his bones and muscles but he was driven on, partly from the simple wish to escape his slavery, partly owing to a sense of obligation to Banks. They had practiced whistles so they could find each other near the river, but Garrad listened in vain for a reply. He became painfully aware of time slipping by and dawn arriving when Makepeace would quickly realize he had gone.

Finally he heard a faint whistle. Unsure if it was a bird greeting the dawn or if it was indeed the Colonel, he worked his way downstream until there, under a sagging tree, he saw Colonel Banks readying the raft to set sail.

Without speaking, Banks indicated that Garrad was to take charge of the oar he had fashioned and to step aboard the craft which was a stout, lumbering contraption of logs held together with bits of string, rope, wire and vines that Banks had collected over the months.

With a nod from Banks they pushed off and drifted out into the channel which was moving fast with the tide. Fearing that they might be seen from the banks of the river, they lay low, drifting on the current and tide with Banks using his oar as a rudder.

After an hour they were clear into the bay and started rowing towards the rocky headland to the southeast where they hoped to pick up a west wind. As they approached the headland the sea picked up quite a chop and this alarmed Banks. Garrad, however, was used to the treacherous waters around the Essex coastline. Calmly, he raised what passed for a sail on the vessel, a stained bed sheet strung between two boards. As the breeze picked up and Garrad felt the strain of the sail holding the wind and saw the water starting to stream by, his spirits rose. Insane as this venture was, it just might work. Cold, hungry and tired as he was, he took some comfort in the fact that it was a tiredness, coldness and hunger that was brought on by his quest for freedom. Garrad nodded to Banks as if to say, "This is good," and set his eyes on the horizon and the coastline.

"At this rate, if everything holds, we will be miles away by sunrise. You did well Colonel," called out Garrad who was feeling invigorated by the salt spray. "You did well in the building of this craft. She seems to be holding up well, but we should still stay within swimming distance of the shore, I think."

"Aye aye captain," replied Banks. "But I fear I cannot swim. Also, I seem to be coming down with *mal de mer*, but no matter."

Garrad looked puzzled. "Sea sickness!" Banks clarified.

VI

They sailed on all day and as evening drew in they pulled into a small cove with a sandy beach to rest up for the night and carry out repairs on the raft. As they hauled up onto the beach, Banks said, "I believe we have put a few miles between us and our keepers."

"Yes," replied Garrad, "But I think we shall have to endure the cold night without a fire."

"Indeed, we do not want to attract attention. I will forage on yonder rocks if you fashion some sort of shelter," replied Banks.

"Good," replied Garrad and he looked around at the trees encroaching on the beach for a good spot. Shortly, he found a rock overhang close to the edge of the small cove and leaned branches and leaves so as to create as much cover as possible. Soon Banks returned with a good haul—limpets, crabs, and a bunch of seaweed.

They shivered incessantly throughout the night and as soon as an iron grey light seemed to emanate from the east and they could discern the vague adumbration of the horizon, they lugged the raft into the water again. Mercifully the tide was up and ebbing so the vessel was soon in the water and with several minutes of pained rowing they were clear of the headland and sailing still east with a sturdy following wind.

They had eaten more than usual during their overnight stay in the cove. It was not over-picked as it was where they were held captive. They were able to relax somewhat, merely keeping an eye on the makeshift sail and the coastline to ensure that they were not too distant from the shoreline.

Garrad almost dozed off. But he was sharply awoken when Banks said, "I fear we may be driven onto that reef ahead." Garrad immediately sensed what was up. The wind had dropped. The tide had changed and they were being carried along inexorably toward a rocky barrier that stood in front of them.

"Quick! The oars!" exclaimed Garrad. They grabbed the oars awkwardly, not wanting to tip the raft in the ever-roughening sea. As they turned to take up their rowing positions, they looked behind. Both of their hearts sank as if united, for there, under full sail, in hot pursuit, was a large grey-brown ship, bearing down upon them.

Stunned, they soon realized their predicament. To row away from the reef was to row to their pursuing captors. To not row meant their raft would be rent to shreds on the rocks. Already they could hear the waves crashing on the blackened, jagged and broken teeth that seemed to gnash the swell and spume around them.

They drifted in the vain hope that they would somehow survive the crashing reef and that the ship would not venture close for fear of being dashed to pieces itself. However the ship loosed a maneuverable dory with four oarsmen who set out speedily across the waters as the ship itself came about.

"Probably whalers," murmured Banks, "They seem to know their stuff."

In what seemed no time, the dory was in hailing distance.

"You have your choice mates," called out the cox. "Either die here on these rocks in a very few minutes or try your luck on Norfolk Island. As for me, this will probably earn me my freedom."

"Sorry old chap. I cannot swim. We will get another chance," said Banks to Garrad who nodded in assent.

"Throw us a rope," called out Garrad, sensing that Banks had a deep resolve and that this was but one in a series of escape attempts he intended.

The cox threw a rope and they were dragged behind the dory, the rowers calling out curses as they labored hard against the swell. Finally they were hauled on board where they were greeted by the gloating Makepeace.

"If I wasn't so sick, I would beat you bloody. But you are fortunate. A ship bearing new convicts, new meat, came yesterday, so I have your replacements. Yes mateys, its Norfolk Island for you. You'll never escape there and you will never begin to earn your freedom like these lads did today. In fact, you will not see out the year." At this Makepeace smiled and snorted.

VII

Garrad and Banks were taken back to the settlement and consigned to the fetid holding pen with two other shabby miscreants. The next morning they were roped together and led off to the waiting boat that ferried them out to the waiting ship. There, they were chained around the base of the forecastle.

"So's I can keep an eye on yer!" explained the captain. "We'll haul anchor at the turning of the tide. We shall stop off at Botany Bay to pick up some other ne'er-do-wells and then, my doves, 'tis off to Norfolk Island, where you will, no doubt, see out your days, such as they are." At this one of the mates chortled, only to be greeted by a stern look from the captain. "When I want your opinion, Shaw, I shall ask for it, if you please! See to those sheets!'

"Aye aye Captain," replied the chastened Shaw.

The tide turned, the wind stiffened and the ship, "The Firebrand", set sail. As it cleared the headland the westerlies picked up apace and full sails were set as the ship ploughed along the southern shore of Tasmania.

"She sails well, don't she?" asked Shaw of the four convicts who were regularly being doused by the spray.

Only Garrad responded. He was forced to admit it was a fine ship. Shaw surveyed the unhappy quartet, emaciated, ragged and in the deepest despair. Suddenly a thought took him.

He went below for a moment and returned with a large, heavy, horsehair blanket that, infested and malodorous as it was, he placed over the four as best he could. Garrad weighed the stink against the warmth and cover provided against the threat of infection and decided that the comfort won out.

"Thanks," he said to Shaw, who was looking on approvingly, as if thinking he had done his Christian duty for the day.

"Can't have you dying off before we get you to Norfolk," he said and then resumed his puttering on the deck.

Three days later they picked up at first a slight change in the smell of the air. The gulls following the ship became more numerous and the ocean made a slightly different sound, had a slightly different feel. Garrad, from his days sailing around the treacherous Essex coast, picked up these things before the other convicts. Soon the hills surrounding Botany Bay were smudgily outlined in ochre and grey against the sky.

"Usually," Garrad thought, "the end of a trip is greeted with some satisfaction, some sense of completion. All I feel at the sight of this beautiful harbor is despair."

He nudged Banks at his side and he and the other two roused themselves from the starvation and misery-induced slumber to survey the approaching continent of Australia.

"Aye," said Shaw, picking up on their fascination, "She is beautiful, isn't she? It's a shame how we must keep the French out by filling it with the likes of you. We shall be here a week while they round up and collect the others here who are bound for Norfolk. You will like your little pen here. It gets hot during the day and cold at night, but a change is as good as a rest." Amused at his own pleasantry, he then set about more deck chores.

Chapter 6

I

The gulls squawked raucously as they bobbed and dived for the slops being thrown overboard by the sailors. Rose, Evangelinha and Mr. Chowdary stood gazing upon the mist-shrouded shore of Brazil. Already they could make out the two tiers of the port of Bahia. The quayside, nestled at the base of some steep bluffs, was busy, full of heavily-laden ships and buzzing with activity like an ants nest. Up above, they could make out the residential aspect of the city, already starting to gleam in the morning sun.

"Ah! It is so good to be home again," murmured Evangelinha. "It has been three years. Too long. Mr. Chowdary, I am sure you will find much to engage your interest here in Salvador. It is a very spiritual place."

"I can feel it already," said Mr. Chowdary.

Rose was quiet throughout this conversation and must have tensed, for Mr. Chowdary, perhaps noticing her tightened grip on the railing, said, "I am sure all will be well Miss Rose. You will find a boat for Australasia and you will be reunited with your beloved Garrad. You know, once you were one soul and you will be reunited. I can see you have very strong karmas over each other."

Rose smiled and seemed to relax. She said, "Thank you Mr. Chowdary. Your words are indeed a comfort and reassurance. But first I must find a ship to transport me."

"First," interjected Evangelinha, "You must stay with me and my family and find your land-legs. We live up there," and she pointed to the crest of the scarp that was by now becoming well defined in the warmth of the morning light, "In the Pelourinho, near the Praça do Se. You must meet my family. They will be so excited to meet an English lady."

"No lady, I am sure, just an ordinary girl…."

"This is of no account. This does not speak to your soul," interjected Mr. Chowdary, smiling.

Soon the ship was heaving to the dock. Ropes were tossed and fastened amid the hurly burly of the wharf. Strange and delicious smells of cocoa, sugars and fruits wafted from every direction as Rose followed Evangelinha to where they took a carriage that slowly, laboriously took them along the zigzag track up the steep escarpment, through the blue painted and tiled houses to where they finally entered a thick mahogany gateway opening into a large courtyard.

Liveried servants came out and helped them down from the carriage and Rose stood by as Evangelinha hugged and kissed several people, most of whom cried and held her face in their hands. Finally Evangelinha introduced Rose and Mr. Chowdary.

"This is my father and this is my brother," and the two men both bowed courteously.

"Dom Machado," said the father, who was slim, tanned and smiled through a well-trimmed moustache and beard.

"And this is my son, Heitor." And the son, tall, trim and somewhat gaunt, bowed in his turn.

"Enchanted, mademoiselle."

"Welcome." Clipped the father, and with a gesture indicated that all three were to be shown to their rooms.

Rose was astonished at the luxuriance of the woods that had been used in the building. Everywhere deep reds and chocolate browns of floors, doors and panels, woods of colours and grains that she had never seen before. It was all she could do not to run her hand over the silky luxuriance. She wanted to pause and take in the coolness of the thick white plastering on the walls and the vivid blue tile trim.

Finally the servant ushered her into her room which was high-ceilinged, furnished again in the lush woods that, she imagined, came from the deep forests of the hinterlands. The window gave brightly onto the courtyard and she looked out and could see that Evangelinha's crates and cases were being unloaded. She also saw two magnificent parrots, one crimson, the other iridescent blue, calmly preening in the shade of the courtyard. She sighed at the luxury, calmness and sense of relaxed abundance. Immediately she became aware that this joy was to be short-lived for she must set about finding passage to Australia.

She heard someone clearing their throat behind her. Turning, she saw Dom Machado.

"I apologize profusely for the intrusion," he said. "My daughter has told me of your situation. Please allow me to be of assistance, especially since I feel that the English will be of great assistance to my people in Portugal in the coming years. Besides, I am a romantic. Tomorrow, if you are up to it, we will visit some of the sites of Bahia and, in addition,

113

get you passage to Australia, although, given your great beauty, we would love to have you stay."

At this, Evangelinha entered, and, having caught the last remark said, "Father! You are shameless! I apologize for this old brigand," she directed to Rose. "The best I can say in his defense is that his heart has been broken since our dear mother's death and with it, apparently, his sense of propriety."

"It is no matter at all. I think I understand, for I myself am bereft without my Garrad. It quite unhinges one," replied Rose, attempting to smooth the waters.

"Anyway, dinner will be in one hour, and," gesturing the maid to enter the room, "here are some clothes more suited to Bahia. Please enjoy them in good health."

"I am so grateful for all your kindnesses. One day, I hope to repay you."

"Find your Garrad and then let us know. That will be repayment enough," replied Evangelinha.

II

"My brother, Heitor, and I think it would serve you well to visit Nosso Senhor de Bonfim," announced Evangelinha at breakfast. "Mr. Chowdary, I think you too would be very interested."

Mr. Chowdary nodded and said, "I trust your judgment, mademoiselle."

"What is it?" inquired Rose.

"It is a church, founded by a man who, while drowning at sea, swore to God that he would build a church if he was saved. He was saved and so he built this church. It is said that if you make a wish there, and make a donation, that wish will come true."

"It was built by slaves and they were sure to put their icons hidden behind the Christian icons so that when they worshipped the slave-owner's God, and Jesus and Mary, they were also, in secret, worshipping their idols of Macumba or Xangu," interceded Evangelinha.

"That would be a powerful mixture," murmured Mr. Chowdary, "But you must always be careful with magic and its temptations."

"I think we all know what wish you will make, Rose," said Evangelinha as Rose nodded, "But I think both the men of this house will be sorry to see you go. I think they are both quite, what is the word, smitten, by you."

Rose and Heitor blushed. Despite the splendor of her surroundings, the fine wafting aromas from the kitchens and the courtyard and the bright crisp light, she did not waver in her resolve to be reunited with Garrad.

III

The carriage pulled up to the church, Nosso Senhor de Bonfim, which was quite small and white, gleaming in the mid-morning sun. A crowd of hundreds was clustered around and as soon as Rose, Evangelinha, Mr. Chowdary and Heitor descended from the carriage they were assailed by a throng of vendors, selling knick-knacks. Some were little girls holding bunches of short thin ribbons.

"Dar me um beijo!" called girl after girl as they offered their cheeks.

"Nom obrigado," said Evangelinha with a smile. "But I think," she said to Rose, "that you might wish to purchase one."

Rose looked puzzled. "A ribbon?"

"Yes, you give the girl a kiss on the cheek and make a wish. She ties the small ribbon around your wrist and you must never take it off. By the time it wears off, your wish will come true."

"You know, I might just give that a try," said Rose and she beckoned to one of the dusky skinned girls that she was ready to give a light kiss on the cheek and have a ribbon, a bright blue one, tied around her wrist.

"Mr. Chowdary, what do you think of such antics?" asked Heitor.

"It is harmless, just so long as we regard it as an entertainment. If we take it for the true path, this, like all magic, will simply lead us astray," replied Mr. Chowdary with a smile as he looked up admiringly at the white edifice of the church.

"More things in heaven and earth," joked Evangelinha.

"Indeed Mademoiselle," assented Mr. Chowdary.

Rose by now had the ribbon tied around her wrist and was looking at it from several angles.

"No doubt as to what you wished for," said Evangelinha knowingly and Rose smiled.

"Shall we go in?' asked Heitor, gesturing towards the thick doors.

It was crowded inside, not only with people, but also with wax impressions of every imaginable body part—legs, feet, jaws, buttocks, heads—leaning up against the walls and hanging from the ceilings on strings and wires.

Sensing Rose's confusion, Heitor explained, "People who are ill make a wax impression of the offending part of their body, bring it here, make an offering in hopes that their prayers will be answered and that they will be cured. The offertory is over there."

Rose and Evangelinha's eyes met and Evangelinha nodded in encouragement. "Make a wish as you make the offering. Here, use this coin, pray deeply, and it will come true. I myself have had some odd things happen as a result of this. Many times I was not at all ready for the fulfillment of the dream."

Rose took the copper coin from Evangelinha and made her way through the crowd around the wooden box. She dropped the coin in and closed her eyes, wishing and praying.

"You are invoking at least two powerful religions here," explained Heitor. "Over there is the statue of Mary but behind her hidden in the wall, the slaves put images of Ijimenha, their sea-goddess. Behind the statue of Jesus on the cross is the slaves' Oxala, and of course when they are praying to Almighty God, they are, in their hearts, praying to Oxum."

"My goodness," said Rose, almost sensing some of the power of this.

"We must be careful what we wish and pray for," murmured Mr. Chowdary. "A person must not be given blessings or knowledge that are too far ahead of their spiritual development."

"I couldn't agree more, Mr. Chowdary," intervened Heitor, "Miss Rose, may I be permitted to take you by the arm and show you a rather splendid view of the ocean?"

"Why thank you sir, of course," replied Rose. As the two walked away, Evangelinha and Mr. Chowdary exchanged glances.

"Be careful of your footing," enjoined Heitor as they approached the lookout point.

"Thank you, sir," replied Rose. "My! The panorama is stunning here. I quail at the enormity of the ocean, and to think I must venture out upon it once more…"

"Indeed," responded Heitor. "Your Garrad is so fortunate to have one so devoted in quest of him."

"I assure you, I have no choice. Without him, I find that my life-force simply shrivels away and I become like a walking ghost. It is unbearable."

"Ah, I think I understand this feeling. But you English are so very odd. I spent a year or so in London and I was and remain puzzled by your twin nature. On the one hand, you are so prim and proper and yet you manage to produce such passionate people. Look at Shakespeare, look at Mr. Donne…"

Rose felt as though she had been struck by a lightning bolt for the mention of the poet's name brought back to her the profound tie that she felt with Lady Catherine and their shared admiration for him.

"I am sorry. Did I say something?' inquired Heitor tentatively, noticing Rose's discomfiture and pallor.

"Oh no…it is just…Donne…I…" and her eyes began to well up.

"I apologize. I am too clumsy."

"No not at all. You are correct," managed Rose as she regained her composure.

"Correct," continued Rose, gathering her scattered thoughts and feelings together. "Mr. Donne has a most excellent way of combing the two, that is of combining cool thought and metaphor with the deepest heartrending passions. I used to share in readings of him with my Ladyship back in Pyefleet."

"Ah. Yes. Of course, and to share such a thing is to be very close with them. I can see how this would be moving. You must miss her."

"I do indeed, sir."

"Please, Heitor."

"Heitor."

"Excellent. I have enjoyed our little promenade and I am grateful for your sharing your reminiscences with me. Is it too forward of me to say that, even though we have only spoken briefly, I feel we have much in common? I am quite lonely here. Not many have heard of Donne, for example. I shall miss your company."

Rose felt her cheeks reddening but was able to manage, "Thank you, Heitor. You and your family are most kind."

"And I think the others are waiting for us," responded Heitor.

IV

Evangelinha, Rose, Heitor and Mr. Chowdary had just retired from the breakfast room to the airy sitting room when Dom Machado entered and said, "I have found just the ship for you, Mademoiselle Rose! It leaves for Botany Bay in two days. It is an English ship putting in here for resupply. From Portsmouth. It has supplies and equipment for the colonists there. I am afraid it is not much of a vessel, but then, you seem determined to reach your beloved."

"Wonderful! Well done father!" exclaimed Evangelinha. Mr. Chowdary nodded as if he had seen it coming all along, Heitor was quite muted in his response, and he asked, "I hope we may still visit the plantation?"

"Oh Heitor, don't be so silly!" exclaimed Evangelinha. "There are oceans of preparation to do." Heitor looked crestfallen so Rose, as if to cheer him up, said, "Perhaps we can fit in a short visit."

"Very well then," replied Evangelinha, "But we must leave shortly. Again, well done father. This is so exciting. Rose, aren't you excited? Or afraid?"

"Much of everything, I think."

"So, it's decided then," said Dom Machado briskly. "I shall secure your passage this afternoon, and in two days you will be catching the westerlies to the Cape of Good Hope."

V

The track to the cacao plantation was rutted and steep. By the time Rose, Heitor, Mr. Chowdary and Evangelinha arrived it was mid-afternoon. It was suffocatingly hot and they were coated in a fine film of red dust. They descended stiffly from the carriage and were led by three burly workers to a shelter where a table had been set with lunch—a thick stew of black beans and pork and roasted fish accompanied by all sorts of fruits the like of which Rose had never seen before.

After the meal, Evangelinha and Mr. Chowdary decided to retire to day beds under a massive shade tree across the clearing. Heitor asked Rose if she would like to see an impressive vista. She, sensing that this was important to him, agreed, even though she was bone-tired and anxiously anticipating her long sea voyage.

Heitor led the way, occasionally holding back the overhanging braches and offering an arm where the ground was slippery underfoot. Finally, the forest gave way to a cleared meadow which they crossed. At the other end the ground dropped away surprisingly steeply and opened up onto a breathtaking vista, lush and green with folded slopes giving way to blue misty shrouds around the verdant curves of the hills. It was as if the leaves sparkled every now and then in the sun and once in a while a brightly coloured bird, now crimson, now emerald green, now sapphire blue, flapped, flitted and fluttered across the canopy.

"Goodness!" exclaimed Rose, "That is quite breath-taking."

"Isn't it?" replied Heitor. "I was hoping you would like it. I love to come here to remind myself that life is worthwhile."

"Goodness, you sound sad," replied Rose.

"I am. I am incomplete. I suffer from a chronic emptiness, as if there is a hole inside of me."

Rose felt at something of a loss with this unexpected intimacy. It was not the kind of conversation she was used to having. "I am so sorry to hear that. I don't know exactly what that is like…but perhaps I do, I lost my parents."

"Ah. You are such a beautiful soul, and if you do not consider it too forward, may I say, a beautiful person," said Heitor and he looked into Rose's eyes. It seemed to her that his eyes had become moist.

"Why thank you," replied Rose.

"And I was wondering, and I know I will be seen as incongruous and importunate, if you could possibly delay your departure for a while. Ships come through frequently. There is so much to see. I feel the emptiness inside me evaporating when you are near me," and at this Rose was certain she heard a slight catch in his voice as his heart was opening and a small tear formed in his eye. "I would give you everything," he said and at this he made a slight gesture with his arms to the vista and then to himself.

Rose herself started to tear up as she seemed to absorb Heitor's emotions. She took a moment or two to collect her thoughts and feelings and finally was able to come out with, "But, I have to go...."

Heitor understood immediately, "Yes, I understand completely. You must find your Garrad. I apologize profusely for being such a, what is the word? Oaf. Please forgive me."

"None needed, Heitor," said Rose, "I am honoured indeed to have been shown these beautiful sights, both this beautiful view," and she gestured to the vista, "and of your deepest longings. I know that you will one day find what you are looking for."

Heitor smiled and gave a short, ironic, bitter laugh. He sighed and then said, "Let us return?"

On the way back, on the bumpy dusty carriage ride, Heitor asked Mr. Chowdary, "There is a philosopher, Mr. Chowdary, who says that we are unfortunate indeed for being alive and that we would be better off never having been born, to just have stayed in oblivion. What do you think of that?"

"This sounds like a man who has wandered off the pathway of spiritual development," replied Mr. Chowdary.

"There is a path?" inquired Heitor. "I must admit, I am more persuaded by the negative."

"Strait is the gate, brother," chimed in Evangelinha.

"There is indeed, my friend and every step you take forward is matched by a thousand steps towards you from the other end by the Creator," interceded Mr. Chowdary.

"That is quite a generous exchange," replied Heitor.

"Indeed it is. One step is repaid a thousandfold."

At this, the company retired into their thoughts, meditating on the lush countryside and their inner worlds.

VI

The dockside was a seeming chaos of activity as Rose, Evangelinha, Heitor and Mr. Chowdary descended from the carriage next to the ship she was to take to Australia. Just as she was about to step onto the gangplank, Heitor touched her arm and said, "I would like you to wear this. Please, as a token of my thoughts, feelings and wishes for you." He held out a silver chain with a small pendant of silver hanging from it. It was, on closer inspection, a small fist with the thumb protruding between the first and second fingers. "It is a figa," he said. "It is part of the local religion. This one has been blessed by a Mae de Santos, so it has an especial power to keep away evil and summon help. I fear you will need it in the voyage ahead and I sincerely hope it will work for you and your beloved."

Rose sensed how meaningful this was for Heitor, especially since he had only just proposed to her. Her eyes moistened and her voice thickened as her heart swelled into her throat, "Why thank you Heitor. How very kind of you."

"Come now, Heitor," interceded Evangelinha. "Let poor Rose be. She has a long and arduous journey ahead and needs none of your emotion."

"All will be well for you," said Mr. Chowdary. "Of this I am certain. You are following your heart. The heart is the gateway to the soul and the soul can do no evil."

"Thank you all. I just don't know how...." said Rose, welling up with emotion as she realized that she would never again see these true friends.

"Yes, yes. We all wish each other well," said Evangelinha briskly, in an attempt to subdue her own welling emotion.

"And we will see each other again," added Mr. Chowdary. "Perhaps in a different form, so we must try to recognize each other."

Rose stepped carefully up the narrow gangplank onto the deck of the waiting ship. At the top she was greeted by a sailor who ushered her to her quarters, which were low-ceilinged and cramped but comfortable enough. In addition there was a porthole allowing for a view, albeit a constricted one, of the ocean.

There was a tap at the door and as she turned she saw a thin young man in a black suit and stiff white collar. "I am sorry if I startled you in any way, nor do I wish to importune you. Please allow me, however, to introduce myself for I think we shall be neighbours. Parson Prendergast."

"Oh. Of course," replied Rose, who despite having risen above her station in life, still curtseyed as would a scullery maid.

Parson Prendergast raised his eyebrows inquiringly.

"Oh, of course, I have quite forgotten my manners in all the kerfuffle. My name is Rose Flaxman. I am bound for

Australia. I am to find and recover my betrothed, Garrad Hansen who has been wrongly sent there."

"Goodness," replied the Parson, "Quite an adventure, I am sure, and not at all the reason most young ladies go to the antipodes."

"How do you mean, sir?" asked Rose.

"Ah! Well, it is a delicate subject; no doubt one that such a lady of such breeding as yourself would be unaware. Namely, that, er, well, so many women who are sent to the colonies are, or should I say, are seen as, ladies of shall we say…"

"I think I catch your meaning sir, you need go no further," interrupted Rose.

"That is to say, they were sent there for being charged as such or upon their arrival shall be forced into such degradation through no fault of their own."

"Oh my goodness!" exclaimed Rose, her heart sinking once again as she realized what she might be sailing towards.

"Yes, the situation in the colonies is execrable, madam. That is part of my mission, to raise the spirits and the moral code in what seems to have become a hell-hole. I am sorry. I seem to have upset you."

"No sir. I am grateful for your warnings, but I must admit to feeling quite affected by the thought of what my beloved must be enduring," replied Rose attempting to compose herself.

Prendergast inhaled deeply, "Again, I apologize for the intrusion. As usual, I have blundered in too impetuously. I hope you will forgive my clumsiness and that we shall become better acquainted on the journey that lies before us."

"Indeed, sir," smiled Rose, still discomfited.

"I think I feel the ship casting off," exclaimed Prendergast. "You will no doubt wish to wave farewell to your friends in Salvador."

"Yes, indeed, farewell," said Rose, the word farewell echoing through her body, heart and soul like a death-knell.

She found her way up on deck and the boat had already pulled several yards from the dock. There on the dock were her friends; Heitor, Chowdary and Evangelinha. Behind them stood dom Machado who had apparently just joined them to bid a final farewell. She pulled a lace handkerchief from the sleeve of her pale blue dress, the one given to her by Evangelinha, waved it and blew kisses of gratitude with her other hand. The warm westerly breeze picked up minute by minute and soon the steep scarp of Salvador became a shadow on the horizon as Rose set out across the South Atlantic Ocean.

VII

Rose sat on the deck in a chair that the sailors had kindly set for her. Feeling the gentle heat of the sun she watched the rise and fall of the distant horizon and the sea-birds still following the ship. Way up on high, a frigate-bird seemed to hover, motionless just aft of the ship, once in a while adjusting its wings to catch the shifting breeze.

"May I be so bold as to join you?" inquired Parson Prendergast as he stood hesitantly beside her holding a chair he had brought from his cabin.

"Please. Do," replied Rose.

"We make good time," said the Parson, looking up to the stiff sails swollen with the following wind.

"Indeed, but it will still be a long, slow journey."

"We must stop in Cape Town, but the captain tells me we must be sharp about it for our boys have just concluded a decisive battle against the Batavians at Blaauwberg. The Cape Colony belongs to Britain now, but a counter-attack could come at any time."

"Goodness," replied Rose, "Battles and wars all over."

"Indeed," replied the Parson. "Even where we are headed, there are rebellions as the convicts rise up against their keepers and as war is waged against the indigenous population."

Rose tightened her lips and looked out at the horizon.

"I am sorry," said the Parson, "How insensitive of me. Yet again I blunder and raise your concerns. I am sure God is protecting your betrothed. I am sure he is using every ounce of his wisdom to steer clear of trouble."

"And yet," responded Rose, "You seem bent on walking into such difficulties."

"It is my duty. My compeers are quite happy to see out their God-given days preaching from the pulpit in a comfortable country church, but I feel my calling is amongst those who are most benighted."

"Australia. The men and women convicts."

"Not only those, for the overseers are equally lost souls. Both the oppressor and oppressed are lost souls who have wandered from the pathway back to God."

Rose smiled and then looked thoughtful.

"Once again, I must apologize," humbly begged the Parson, "It appears I have unwittingly climbed into the pulpit. You smile is well-deserved."

"Oh, no sir! I was not laughing at you, far from it. I was simply smiling at the thought of your raising the spirits of an entire continent. Your language is rather high-flown for convicts and supposed 'fallen ladies'," replied Rose, adding, "I fear it is I who must apologize now."

"Not in the least!" remonstrated Prendergast. "Your point is well-taken! I must take pains to speak their language and meet them on their level. Here," and he reached inside his coat, "Please read this, it is a new book, by a Miss Louisa Stanhope, or at least I believe her to be a 'Miss'. It is at once edifying and uplifting. It seeks to entertain and to develop the moral spirit of whomsoever should read it. I intend to use it and several other novels in the edification of those held in servitude and their keepers. Please, read it and tell me what you think."

"Why thank you, Parson. I shall read it. It shall help pass the time," replied Rose taking the book.

"Excellent! And when you are done, I have several more. I await your opinion eagerly. At the very least, these books, which are filled with the sights, sounds and smells of our beloved England will help us feel more at home," added the Parson.

At this, they fell silent, Prendergast, feeling comforted at having spread the good word, Rose looking out over the ever-restless ocean, musing on her fate and looking forward to the entertaining pastime of the book Prendergast had given her. She opened the book and read the title and author, "Montbrasil Abbey, by Louisa Stanhope".

VIII

"It is really quite breathtaking, isn't it," said Parson Prendergast as he stepped up to the side of Rose who was gazing at the approaching silhouette of the Cape Colony. The morning sky was azure and spotted with only a few puffs of cumulus and this made the flat top of Table Mountain stand out in stark relief. In the foreground nestled the small settlement of Cape Town.

"Indeed it is. I have mixed feelings. I would be curious to explore but I need to move on speedily," replied Rose.

"Yes, as the captain said, our stay must be a short one for we have only just reclaimed this from the Dutch," said Prendergast.

"So much conflict," mused Rose.

As they approached the port, it became clear that the entire place was bustling with soldiers of all sorts and all the ancillary business of war—provisions were being unloaded at great pace and heavy guns lurched on hoists over the edges of ships and onto the docks where, amid great shouting and remonstrances, they were hauled off.

They finally were able to dock, but when they did an officer yelled from the quayside that they must make haste and be off by the next tide, for more supplies were on their way and were desperately needed. The Batavians were still fighting up-country and threatening attack.

"You may take on fresh water and food, if you may find it, but then you must be on your way!" yelled the officer, making no bones about it.

The captain, ruffled, called back, "So it's martial law then?"

"You might say that, captain. We are at war. We are claiming this for England," he said gesturing widely to include all around, even to the top of Table Mountain. "Also, no one except as are essential to your purposes may come ashore. I am sorry Madame and you too, sir," he said, acknowledging Rose and Parson Prendergast.

"You hear that, my boys! We are at war. Make haste! You men," and he gestured four sailors swabbing the deck, "Fetch water!"

"Aye, aye Captain"

"And, you," pointing at two others, "Provisions!"

IX

Three days out of Cape Town and they were becalmed in the Horse Latitudes. The sea seemed like oil and the air was thick and muggy. On the odd occasion when a breeze struck up it was listless, half-hearted and changed direction in a trice. The sails remained limp and the atmosphere on board was sagged and irritable.

Rose, attempting to keep up her spirits, was standing at the gunwale, alternately looking out to the flat ocean and the ribbon still on her wrist from the little girl in Salvador. It was showing signs of wear, but it seemed as though it would take forever for it to finally wear away and her dream to come true. She felt oppressed by the dull depressive atmosphere on the boat that pressed down upon her as if it was a physical force and she resolved inwardly not to let it infect her spirits. As she did this she found herself fingering the figa that Heitor had given her. She smiled to herself, both at her unwonted superstition and at the tender feelings she harbored for him.

Her smile was interrupted by a resumption of the pained groaning from the cabins below. Several of the men had been overtaken with the most virulent dysentery and their anguished cries only added to the general sense of despair on the vessel.

The Captain yelled down from the forecastle, "Parson Prendergast, will you kindly hasten below to do what you can to offer those men some spiritual comfort? And you miss, might I prevail upon you to look like a nurse and offer them some sweet Godspeed or whatever?"

Prendergast emerged, somewhat ruffled, from his cabin and nodded in assent, as did Rose. They both stepped to the hatchway leading to the fetid stench of below deck where the men lay, their lives draining from them.

"Not that they deserve such comfort," grumbled the captain, to himself, but loud enough so that everyone could hear, "I know they partook of some rotten bush-meat whilst they were ashore at the Cape, supposed to be getting victuals for us all, they fed themselves alright. Now this is their comeuppance. I wish they would just depart quietly and quickly like gentlemen, but no, they have to make a song and dance about it."

As they stepped below Rose and the Parson were physically assailed by the stench. There at the bottom of the stairs they beheld the three sailors, lying on cots. Their faces were waxen yellow and drawn and they seemed to take turns in groaning and writhing in agony. They ranged in age. One was an old salt with long grey wisps of hair matted on his forehead. Another was a middle-aged man with a brutish countenance seemingly defying the death that all seemed to face. The last was a small boy, scarcely ten years old, so young that his voice had not yet broken and his high pitched whimpers stabbed into Rose's heart in their pained innocence.

Both Rose and the Parson stood in stunned, disgusted silence as they beheld the scene. So frequent were the effusions from the sick men and boy that a hole had been cut in their bunks beneath their buttocks so that their diarrhea could flow straight from them into the buckets below.

A fellow sailor took two of the buckets and brushed past Rose and the Parson as he went upstairs to throw them overboard. Rose could not help but look at the bucket, brimming as it was with excrement, blood and pus.

"Aye miss, 'tis the bloody flux. "'Tis just a matter of time now," he said as he made his way up the steps.

Parson Prendergast stepped over to the old man as if to speak to him but quickly realized that he had at that moment slipped into the relief of unconsciousness.

"Oh Lord," he prayed, "Please allow this man, your servant, peace, tranquility and freedom from pain and, if it is your will, receive him into your grace." The old man remained motionless, comatose, but the young boy started wailing even further as stomach cramps wracked his tiny emaciated frame. At this the middle-aged man started flailing about, as if possessed.

"Damn you! Damn your eyes! Curse you and your God and all of your kind!" he screamed out, attempting feebly to get up, looking at Rose and the Parson with glittering, yellow-stained eyes. "Go to hell! All of you!"

As if sensing the man's perturbation the small boy started screaming in terror, as if he was being attacked by some fearful entity himself. The sailors at the other end of the cabin yelled out to keep the noise down, to shut up. One finally called out impatiently, "Die you bastards, die!"

At this moment the sailor returned from above decks with his buckets and said to Prendergast, "Sir, I think it would be well if you were to repair upstairs. I think their minds and spirits are beyond your reach and you are only upsetting them more."

Shaken, Prendergast nodded in assent and gestured Rose to the stairs. She ascended and he followed.

Prendergast strode on wobbling legs to the gunwale and peered over the edge. Rose accompanied him and was at a complete loss as to how she might comfort him for although she was deeply stricken by the tragedy unfolding below deck, he was doubly stricken, for in addition, his powers to minister to the sick and the suffering had failed. He was riven with deep anxiety over the task he had set for himself in Australia.

Later that day, in the unrelenting swelter and the stunned, still sea, both men and the boy finally succumbed.

"Sew them up boys, and not too much ballast to weigh them down. We shall need it in the storms ahead," called out the captain from the forecastle.

Duly the three were sewn into a canvas bag each with a single rock to hasten their descent to the sea bed.

"A lesson for us all," opined the captain. "Just hard tack from now on, if you want to make it to Botany Bay," he added with a dry laugh.

As if mercifully, shortly after, a westerly breeze picked up and the timbers creaked like old arthritic joints as the sails billowed and the ship strained eastwards. Rose felt a curious relief at the sound of the hull slipping and rippling through the water

X

"I have a delicate matter, I would like to discuss with you if you have a moment," inquired Prendergast hesitantly as he stood at the open door of Rose's cabin. She was busy reading one of the books that he had given her, but she stopped, looked up and said, "But of course Parson. Please come in," and she gestured to a seat across from her.

"Thank you. I wonder if it might be seemly for you to refer to me as Miles. That is my Christian name." he said nervously as he sat down. Rose felt she knew what was coming, but resolved to be patient and let it come out, whatever it was.

"But of course. Miles it is," she replied.

"The captain says we are making good time and that we shall be in Botany Bay before we know it," started Prendergast.

"Indeed," responded Rose. "I think we all need this trip to be over, no matter what trials and tribulations await us in Australia."

"Yes, the events have been trying indeed and as to our diet of tack, well…"

"Yes," replied Rose her thoughts and feelings straying sadly to the two men and a boy who succumbed to the bloody flux.

"So I was wondering, being fully aware of your mission to regain contact with your beloved, if, heaven forbid, I do not know how to say this without appearing inconsiderate but my intentions are entirely aimed your well-being for I have come to believe, during our voyage together to come to admire you greatly and would wish you nothing but good—that is, er..." Miles Prendergast was somewhat out of breath and at a loss for words.

Rose rescued him. "It is quite alright Miles, you may say it without hurting my feelings or crushing my dreams. Heaven knows I think of it with the deepest dread every minute. I might not find my Garrad. Australia, as we have seen, is a dangerous and deadly place where his life counts for almost nothing, less than an animal's."

"I know, dreadful thoughts indeed, and I regret from the uttermost depths of my soul that one so noble and gentle as yourself should have to endure such affects, er... But if that was the case and of course I would not for one moment wish it so. If it did turn out that you, due to some tragic and unforeseen and undeserved eventuality, find yourself alone and in need of a partner, for indeed the antipodes, so I hear, is a place where just such a union is of the profoundest necessity, I would be in Botany Bay, attending to the spiritual needs of the men and women and if you, as I say, well, I would be honoured Rose, beyond all belief and recognition if you would consider, even for one moment to join me as a helpmeet. While at the same time, hoping that this would never be so, you understand?" Miles Prendergast looked anxiously and expectantly at Rose.

"I think I understand completely, Miles, and I take your kind offer in the spirit in which it is intended, one of gracious appreciation and kindness. We shall always be fast friends, I believe and I am grateful for that. Also, I must continue my quest for my true love, Garrad. I feel sure he is out there somewhere thinking of me."

"Of course," replied Prendergast. "Excellent. So I think that is settled then? I believe I must stretch my legs a bit on deck. Would you accompany me?"

"Presently, Miles," replied Rose. "I will finish this chapter."

"Ah yes, excellent," replied Prendergast as he stood, straightened his jacket. He bowed ever-so-slightly and feeling an inward sense of relief made his way, swaying with the movement of the ship, to the hatchway. Rose returned to her book with a kindly, placid smile.

Chapter 7

I

The holding pen in which Garrad, Colonel Banks and their two fellow-convicts found themselves was muddy and strewn with fetid pools of excrement. They found a corner that stood on somewhat higher ground and made the best of the situation. It started to get chilly as the sun dipped angrily below the distant hills. At that time a ragged overseer lead an aged convict and a small aborigine boy to the padlocked gate. He undid it and threw the man and kicked the boy inside. The boy, falling, bumped into the older convict who then flew into a rage, cursing the small boy who was about ten years old and less than one third of the man's size.

The man caught the boy and then set about beating him, not just one cuff about the ears but several closed fist punches, followed by multiple kicks. The boy fell to the ground where the man proceeded to kick him yet more, all the time cursing and the boy writhing in agony, blood oozing from his mouth and pouring from his nose.

"I say, steady on old chap!" called out Banks.

"Yeah mate, hold hard, he's but a boy and it was only accident!" joined in Garrad.

"You buggers! I'll do as I please with this black bastard and I don't have to listen to twats such as you," replied the man who seemed demented, so deep was his rage. He resumed kicking the boy who now was almost lifeless.

At this Garrad and Banks hoisted their aching bodies and started over to the other side of the pen. Their two companions, exhausted from illness and starvation simply waved their hands in wan encouragement.

The man swung wildly at Banks but he, who, it turned out, had had some boxing training was able to avoid the blows with deft footwork. Garrad meanwhile slipped behind the man and, using the strength still remaining after years of handling horses, was able to restrain him.

At this point Banks started to reason with the madman.

"Look," he said, "We have you at our mercy. You are restrained and I am able to hit you at will." The man struggled haplessly against Garrad's still anvil-like body. "So, let us call it a day, shall we? I suggest the young chap accompanies us over there and that shall be your spot over there and we shall pass this delightful night as amicably as possible. What do you say?"

"You will pay for this. You will pay sorely! Not just from me when I get the chance, but from them." He spat in the direction of the boy. "If you show them any kindness, they will up against you."

"Well. We shall see about that," replied Banks. "I think he might turn out to be the perfect gentleman," he added with an ironic smile. "What do you say? Peaceful co-existence?"

The convict grunted. Banks and Garrad nodded to each other. Garrad released the fellow who then shrugged and half sauntered, half limped off to the far corner of the pen.

"Come with us, old chap," said Banks. The boy did not fully understand. Garrad gestured that he was to follow them, saying, "It will be alright," and the three walked back carefully across the mud and slime, avoiding the puddles to the somewhat drier corner where the other two convicts sat, sagging and blank-faced.

A small group of overseers and freedmen had gathered outside the pen, for this was rare entertainment. Unnoticed by anyone, hidden behind the nearby trees, stood the father of the boy who witnessed the whole performance. Inwardly this man made a resolve.

II

The night was chill, damp and dark, so neither Garrad nor Banks were fully asleep, only drowsy, when they heard a double snipping sound to their left. This was followed by a hiss and then two curt short whispers, one from the boy whom they had rescued from the beating the previous evening and the other from a thin figure they could barely make out. The boy reached over in the blackness and tugged on Garrad's sleeve. As if by telepathy he caught on to what was happening and tugged on Bank's sleeve. With the gaunt figure of the aboriginal father holding open the gaping hole in the fence with one hand, whilst holding a pair of old rusty pincers in the other and crouching watchfully above them, they started to crawl out of the pen. Banks gestured to their other two fellow travellers, but they lay lifeless, unaware in the slightest degree of what was happening. They were probably done for as it was and they certainly could not keep up in the arduous trek that no doubt lay before them. Reluctantly, Banks decided to slip through the hole.

No sooner had he made this resolution than there was a crack from where the guard sat on duty. They all froze, wishing and hoping for invisibility. A full minute passed thus with no further sound. They all pushed through the hole in the fence and stepped lightly, following the older aboriginal's footsteps to the perimeter of the settlement, careful to avoid lighting and dogs. Eventually, they made the forest that enveloped the settlement and paused. Garrad and Banks assumed that they would part ways but the older man, whom they could now make out, bone-thin, grizzled and yet superbly flexible and athletic, managed to communicate through gestures that he loved the young boy dearly. Garrad and Banks surmised he was his father. He then indicated that he was grateful to Garrad and Banks and that they should follow him, that they would be welcome and he would find them food and lead them to freedom. Surprised both at the man's largesse and at the complexity of the message he had managed to wordlessly deliver, both Garrad and Banks nodded in eager assent, for they were completely lost. The time had come for the sharing of names.

"Gigby. Magaw," said the old man, pointing first to himself and then to his son. Garrad could not help but think that these were but their versions of names bestowed on them by the colonials and being used out of politeness and convenience.

"Garrad. Banks," offered Garrad, pointing to himself and his companion.

With a nod, Gigby indicated that were to follow him and he set off into the deep forest, noiselessly and at a brisk pace. Soon, they found themselves in what, at first blush, looked to be dense undergrowth, impassable jungle and tangle of thorn and vine. However, it turned out to be, with Gigby's deft footwork, a weaving narrow pathway that lead them ever further away from the camp.

Exhausted as they were, they pressed on. Soon, they started to climb and at glorious intervals as they started to climb the hills surrounding the bay, they caught the panorama of the ocean, now being touched by the first light of dawn. But they did not tarry long. By now the alarm would be set in the camp and there would be hunting parties and dogs set loose. They kept slogging on.

III

The first signs of dawn were signaled by the occasional glimpses they had of high wisps of cirrus cloud turning pink. Soon, as they came upon a small crystal-clear spring, Gigby signed that they should stop. They all drank vigorously, Gigby and Magaw deferentially letting Garrad and Banks go first. Then Gigby and his son motioned for Banks and Garrad to sit down and they disappeared, as if dissolving, into the bush leaving Garrad and Banks prostrate on the ground, exhausted and famished, but feeling a deep contentment while still alert for any sound of approaching dogs or men.

Around them, the forest was waking up. At first there were squawks, squeaks and laughing chatter from birds assertively announcing their presence, then, as it started to get warmer, insects started humming and buzzing in different tonalities. Suddenly, silently, Gigby and Magaw appeared bearing fronds of leaves, bouquets of red berries and a leaf folded cleverly that contained several fat grubs. Apparently, they had eaten while they gathered for they gestured for Garrad and Banks to eat their fill.

Garrad and Banks hesitated but a moment, so profound was their hunger. With the large, fat white grubs, however, they did pause longer until an encouraging nod and smile from Gigby persuaded them to swallow the thing whole. Almost immediately they felt as if every cell in their body gave thanks for the nourishment that seemed to flow instantaneously into their flesh. The meal consumed, they both took deep breaths and smiled at their guides with heartfelt gratitude. They felt buoyed up with hope that this time they might well escape.

Before they got up to leave, however, Gigby picked a bunch of leaves from a nearby bush. He screwed them up in his fists and soaked them in the spring water. Then gesturing Garrad to approach, he applied the leaves to Garrad's still festering shoulders. Garrad felt a tingling and then a numbness, then a deep cleansing and itching sensation. He smiled. Gigby smiled in recognition of Garrad's sense of relief. He picked another frond of the leaves and gave it to Garrad for later use.

It was time to move on. The land was getting yet more hilly and every now and then when there was a clearing in the forest and undergrowth, Garrad could see ahead. In front of them were mountains. He could make out blue limned ridges, deep velvety-green forested valleys out of which arose stunning white and cream-coloured scarps. He found it at once beautiful and daunting. At one point, as he and Gigby were gazing upon this jutted range, he looked at his guide questioningly, as if to say, "Are we really going there?" Gigby, picking up the subtlety of the request raised his eyebrows and nodded. Then he pressed on down the narrow pathway which was forever being overgrown by the insistent bush.

IV

Day after day they continued their journey, Gigby and Magaw briskly and nimbly leading the way, forever seeming to disappear into what looked like an impenetrable mass of foliage only to discover what seemed to be a secret pathway leading ever upwards into the mountains.

At each stop, usually by a spring, pool or waterfall Garrad and Banks took pains to learn the foods that they were eating. It seemed that the forest was a veritable garden refulgent with berries, leaves, tubers, roots, eggs, insects and a full complement of animals. Even though their exertions were enormous, Garrad and Banks could feel the strength returning to their bodies. In addition, their wounds were healing thanks to the ministrations of Gigby's medicaments.

Gigby, helpfully, would show Garrad and Banks his ways of finding the path and its markers. He took pains to show them edible and dangerous plants. He showed them how to listen for sounds of the forest that would tell them of nearby resources and dangers. Garrad and Banks were eager learners for they had the presentiment that soon Gigby, having other missions to accomplish, would leave them to their own resources in this vast and strange landscape. Their eagerness to learn was also informed by the deep indebtedness they felt towards the man who had delivered them, out of his own gratitude, to such a peaceful and beautiful place. Day by day they felt their strength returning. Their humor returned and they started to hum songs as they walked in the certainty that they were now well beyond the reach of their captors who knew nothing of these pathways.

Garrad would sing the beautiful melody he had heard Rose play on the piano at Parson Highweather's, "Lowlands Away". As he sang it he felt its many layers of meaning. They were leaving the lowlands of Botany Bay and heading into these cliffed mountains. His spirits were rising and yet in the song, there were terrible dreams of the death of one's beloved. The song came from deep, deep inside.

> "I dreamed a dream, the other night.
> Lowlands, lowlands away my love.
> I dreamed my love she was dead and gone.
> Lowlands, my lowlands, away."

It must have been that the poignant, bittersweet, melancholy strains caught the imagination of his company for soon, after at first faltering, they were all singing robustly this old song as they picked their way along the ancient trackway.

Soon, they found themselves deep in the mountains with deep verdant valleys and shining white and cream coloured cliffs rising above, gleaming in the sun. They threaded their way through the valleys and gorges, sometimes wading along streambeds, forever climbing as the streams flowed against their movement, ever back to the coast. The streams, however, got smaller and smaller as they progressed and Garrad believed that this was a sign that they must be nearing the crest of the mountain range. Their diet changed accordingly as the vegetation became somewhat more sparse. Again, Gigby took pains to demonstrate to Banks and Garrad the gathering and preparation of the local pantry.

By now, Gigby must have realized they were well beyond reach of their pursuers for he showed Garrad and Banks how to start a fire using a fire stick and the proper kindling. This was accompanied by incantations that to Garrad, seemed to both encourage the fire and express gratitude for its arrival. When Gigby showed them how to find crayfish in the nearby stream and how to roast them wrapped in leaves with baked tubers, both Garrad and Banks could fully appreciate these songs of praise and gratitude.

They consumed fully the meal, rested and then, feeling heavy with food but strong, they continued along the almost imperceptible pathways. And then, as if in a moment or two, Garrad realized they were now descending, going downslope more than upslope. With a skip in his heart, he asked himself if they could truly have traversed the entire mountain range. Surely, he thought, we must be safe and sound here.

Presently, all four emerged onto a wide, high bluff that overlooked an undulating plain that stretched as far as the eye could see. Green, with patches of ochre and copses of trees and bushes, it seemed calm, warm and welcoming.

"Katoomba," said Gigby, gesturing the expanse with his arm.

"Katoomba," repeated Garrad.

Gigby nodded and then briskly led the group down the hill into the valley below.

Once in the valley, when they reached a river that was lined with lush pasture, they proceeded no more. By a small copse of trees there stood a shelter, oval, some thirty feet by twenty, constructed of multiple interweaving arches of logs and covered with brush. After fifteen minutes of repair, Gigby and Magaw showed the place to be sturdy, weatherproof and comfortable. They started a fire.

Once again Gigby and Magaw showed Garrad and Banks the local larder of foods, this time indicating as best they could that they must soon depart. This deepened Banks' and Garrad's motivation to learn.

Gigby lead them upstream where the river widened and became shallower. There he showed them an arrangement of rocks, curving, coiling and interlacing like a maze across the stream. Gigby then waded out to one of the pools created in the middle of the stream and with a few deft strokes pulled out three stout speckled trout.

"As fine a fish trap as I ever saw!" exclaimed Garrad.

After wading back to the bank and throwing them on the grass, Gigby stepped back and started to gather crayfish. He beckoned to Garrad and Banks to join him in his hunt. After a short while they headed back to the shelter, stoked the fire and ate a splendid meal of baked fish, crayfish and roasted tubers.

Afterwards they found some same shade under a nearby aromatic tree and as they dozed off, Garrad and Banks felt confident they could survive here. They had been eager students and Gigby and Magaw, excellent teachers.

After several days, early in the morning, a group of twelve of Gigby's group arrived. They greeted each other joyously, shared food and stories and then Gigby walked up to Garrad and Banks and indicated that he must leave but that he would return in several days' time. He reassured himself that Garrad and Banks knew how to feed themselves for that time and cracked a joke or two about not eating certain leaves that induced diarrhea. Then the group walked off and within a minute or two, as if by magic, they disappeared, as if vaporized.

V

And so the days passed. Garrad and Banks managed to pry some fish from the fish trap and capture the crayfish that seemed to be in an endless supply in the river and adjoining streams. They were able to remember enough of what Gigby had taught them to find tubers, leaves and berries to sustain themselves well. They were careful to keep the fire going for they did not trust their ability to start another. Much of their day was spent in repose and in attempting to pass the time in conversation.

"Eggs!" announced Banks one bright morning as he returned from one of his forays.

"Not too far along, I hope," replied Garrad.

"No, I've been watching the nest. They are fresh. I took four and left three. I'll wrap them in those leaves."

Banks poked at the fire and carefully placed a couple of logs on to keep it going. He looked around and said, "You know, this is a truly remarkable place. The grass is as lush and verdant as the South Downs. The river is full of fish and crustaceans. So many of the plants are edible. This could be paradise."

"Yes, but I still miss my Essex marshes, friends and of course…"

"Yes, quite," interrupted Banks, seeing that Garrad was quite close to tearing up. "I miss my horses, they would do very well here, I think. I can see it, a little cottage up there on that hill, pastures sweeping down to the stream. Maybe a wife and children…"

"A little plot of England on this faraway shore?" asked Garrad with a smile.

"Yes, quite," replied Banks. "A few more of us and I think we would completely bugger the whole thing up. But it is truly spectacular. Sometimes, time seems to stand still. One feels as if one has been here forever." Banks took a few steps over to a large fallen log that served as their seat and plumped down. No sooner had he sat than a brown and gold viper darted out from under the log and sank its fangs into his calf. Banks grimaced and shuddered. The snake held fast, writhing as if to be sure its venom would dig deeper into its victim. Garrad started up and in a few paces was at Banks' side. He managed to grab the viper's tail, wrench it loose, swing it around and whip it against the log until it was smashed and dead. This done, he returned his attention to Banks, who was already lying on the ground, quivering in shock from the toxins. Garrad took off his ragged shirt and tied it as a tourniquet just above Banks' knee. He squeezed at the two bloody points of the bit in vain hope of suppurating the venom. Very quickly Banks started to contort and jolt as if in a fit. He started to lose consciousness and his breathing became stertorous. He attempted to speak but could only manage a whisper. Garrad lowered his head to Banks face.

"Done for…" Banks gasped, "freedman in year…take my name."

Shortly after this, Banks mercifully lost consciousness. Before noon, he was dead.

Devastated, Garrad spent the next few days burying his friend. A hundred yards away from the camp some subsidence had created a small pit, some ten by eight feet. Garrad placed Banks' body in it, wrapped in as many broad leaves and fronds as he could find. He painstakingly gathered together handful upon handful of clods of earth that he pried from the river bank. When the grave was level he gathered together a heap of boulders from the stream bed and built a sort of cairn. On top, he placed a cross, fashioned from two logs and held together with strips of tree bark. On it, with a sharp stone and a burning ember, he scratched and etched an inscription. He improvised a small ceremony. When it was done, he took a deep breath and turned back to his camp, heavy with the blank realization that he had to face the remainder of his days alone.

Chapter 8

I

A fine, misty rain was settling on the docks and the settlement of Botany Bay as Rose's ship quietly slid towards the quayside. In some way she was comforted by the weather, for it reminded her of the mists that would roll in off the North Sea onto her beloved Essex marshes that would trickle and tinkle with the turning of the tide, much as the waters rippled and ruffled as the boat hove to.

Her mood, however, soon became bleak and deeply pained when she beheld the sorry scene on the docks—men in chains, starving, and men harnessed like beasts of burden, cursings of all kinds and whips, lashes and oozing wounds seemingly everywhere. At the foot of the quayside was a pen holding a half a dozen men, who positively sagged under the burden of starvation, fatigue and illness. In front of a makeshift warehouse she saw two bodies, barely clothed, lying in the rain, dead and useless, waiting for someone to bother to dispose of them like so much rubbish. Her heart contracted and tears welled up as she realized that this was Garrad's fate.

"He is strong," she told herself. "He could survive this. He must survive this."

Prendergast, sensing the forlorn meanness of the situation they surveyed, stepped to her side and said, "I believe it would be best if you accompanied me. This environment seems hostile to a lady of delicate sensitivities."

"Thank you, Parson. I believe you are correct," she replied, summoning up her inner strength.

As they walked down the quay, they attracted much attention.

"Ah here's the man of God, come to save our souls! Good luck to you sir, for we are truly lost here," cried out one overseer. This elicited a guffaw from another overseer but the convicts were so drained that they gave no reaction.

"And he has brought us a new doxie!"

This last brought another surge of laughter and grunts from the overseers. Rose stiffened and Parson Prendergast offered his arm to her in support and protection. Finally the ribaldry ended as they approached the end of the quay and saw, as if waiting for them, a tall erect, cockaded military man who stiffly tipped his hat to them.

"I apologize for the reception. I am afraid we are too rough here. Perhaps you, Parson and your elegant associate, can bring some much-needed civilization to these, our benighted denizens. Excuse me, I am Captain Lisle."

"Parson Prendergast and this lady is my friend, Miss Rose Flaxman."

"Excellent! May I show you to your lodgings? They have been vacant since the last occupant, a Parson Shearling died of the bloody flux, almost a year ago. He had trouble reaching these men. Fell into despair. Took to drink. You must be very careful, very strong, to survive here. Shall we?" he inquired as he gestured the direction up the muddy pathway between the dank, damp, planked buildings.

II

Finally they reached the house, such as it was—a forlorn, bedraggled mess of slats of wood, loosely nailed and strung together. It stood at the end of a trail that would be by turns muddy and dusty, ensconced in a thicket of now dripping trees on a slight rise, set back and away from the main settlement. Fortunately, there were two bedrooms and, although dusty and cluttered, the stove and implements were in working order.

"I shall select one of the girls to do for you," offered Captain Lisle.

"Oh, that will not be necessary," replied Rose, recalling her previous life as a scullery maid, still finding it odd that she was taken for a lady.

"Oh I assure you, they will be quite happy to work for you. It will be a vast improvement over their current lot."

Rose, sensing that this was indeed the case and resolving to make life as pleasant as possible for her new maid, replied, "Thank you, Captain. That would be perfect."

"Good," he replied briskly, "I shall send her up presently. She can help you get the place cleaned, get you settled in and prepare your first meal."

Parson Prendergast all this time had been looking around his new abode with an attitude of vacancy born of shock and dismay. However, he did finally manage to utter, "Thank you Captain."

"Oh, my pleasure, I assure you. It will be nice to have someone civilized to speak to. Now, as to civilization, I assume being a man of God, you have no weapon?"

"Quite so."

"Nevertheless, the denizens of this hell-hole are often quite dangerous and you, we, will need protection. I will take the liberty of having one of my men furnish you with some protection. Just in case."

"Not necessary, God will…"

"Cromwell old chap! Believe in God, but keep your gunpowder dry, what?" came Captain Lisle's crisp response. "I must beg your leave, madam and Parson. The girl, Elsie, will arrive shortly." With that the Captain turned on his heel and strode off.

"Oh look!" exclaimed Rose, "A piano!" In the corner was an upright gold and brown faded and dusty piano. Hardly believing it would work, Rose lifted the lid and played a scale. It was, to her and the Parson's great surprise, still relatively in tune.

Rose smiled, but the parson was preoccupied.

"You seem downcast," observed Rose.

"I feel defeated," replied Parson Prendergast. "I feel like a mad castaway. I cannot reach anyone. Those men on the ship found me irrelevant, worse, an annoyance! These men here see me as only a target for their jibes. They hate me and all that I stand for. I am afraid I am consorting with the sin of despair. I feel forsaken."

Rose was flummoxed for she felt the depth of Prendergast's anguish and hopelessness. She had felt that way herself so frequently, not only in the last year but also in her childhood. Her mind raced as she searched for some words of true comfort, not just some useless platitude that would simply mimic the uselessness Prendergast felt. Suddenly it came to her, an insight, seeming mad at first but having its own strange logic.

"You are simply feeling what these men feel but cannot say. They are in such deep anguish they have no words for their pain and suffering and so they act upon you with derision and contempt so as to make you feel what they feel. It is their substitute for language. Your task is thus to take your feelings not as your own but as theirs. It comes from them. This is how they feel. It is their way of telling you." Rose faltered at the evanescence of her idea which seemed now clear, now obscured in her thoughts. "I am sorry, it is hard to explain," she said.

Prendergast looked thoughtful, almost as if he wasn't listening at all, as if he thought that these were but deranged maunderings, but then he said, "You are correct. They are telling me how they feel by making me feel it. That's it! Thank you Miss Flaxman, you have provided me with a golden key. I think your concept will work. Hmm!" and he reflected a moment more and then said, "I think we would be wise to start tidying up a bit. Please select the room you would like to occupy."

Rose smiled, for she had already secretly chosen the room that now was lit by the glittering rays of the late afternoon sun. It had finally stopped drizzling.

III

The previous occupant, in his despair, had left the abode in considerable disarray and there was dust everywhere.

However, Rose and Prendergast were able to find all that they needed to settle in—bedding, coverlets, pots, pans and cutlery. Rose found herself calling upon her old skills of a scullery maid as she busied herself getting the place in order and after an hour the abode looked somewhat homey. Parson Prendergast was at a loss and dithered hither and yon. Rose bustled about him as he stood holding a fire iron or a pair of tongs in the middle of the living room.

As she stood outside the front door of the cabin-cum-shack-cum-house, beating a dusty and worn carpet, she glanced down the track whence they had come and saw a tall, thin and stooping individual, hauling a sack and clad in brown and grey, trudging up the still muddy path. As the visitor approached Rose could finally make out that it was a woman.

"My name's Elsie. I'm here to do for you. I was sent by the captain."

"Very good," replied Rose.

"And I've brought some victuals," said Elsie, indicating the sack. "The captain gave me a pot of mutton stew. Shall I get the stove going and cook up a meal for you and the parson?"

"That would be wonderful."

Two hours later and evening had fallen. Elsie had got the stove burning ferociously and prepared a stew. She had cajoled and cursed the lamps into working and the cabin was suffused with a comforting orange glow. Elsie placed two bowls of the steaming mutton stew on the table and prepared to leave.

"No! You must eat with us Elsie. Please, if you would be so kind. We do not take on airs here," insisted Rose.

Elsie hesitated, having clearly learned well the lesson of not rising above her station.

"I too insist, Elsie. Please join us, if you would be so kind. You should partake of the fruits of your labours," added Prendergast.

Elsie fetched a bowl, ladled some of the thick fatty stew into it and sat across from the parson, next to Rose.

"May I lead us in grace?" inquired Prendergast. The two ladies nodded in assent. "For what we are about to receive, may the Lord make us truly thankful."

"Amen," they all quietly nodded in agreement, for it was a moment that was laden with what the parson might call grace, each feeling some sense of arrival and, no matter how tenuous that sense and condition might be, it was to be honoured and savoured in that fleeting moment.

They started eating, slowly at first. The parson and Rose had been on a diet of mostly hard tack since the shipboard outbreak of bloody flux and their stomachs were still attuned to the sea motion they had been experienced for months. Elsie seemed to keep pace with them out of politeness.

Eventually, it was the parson, eager to reach out to his new congregation, who broke the silence.

"This place surely tests the body and the spirit," he offered.

"Oh indeed, sir. I have been here six months and I cannot bring myself to describe the brutality I have encountered for fear of discomfiting you and your ladyship and for fear of becoming overwhelmed with sorrow myself."

"Please, call me Rose, or Miss Flaxman. As to your experiences I would hope you would feel free to describe them. Sometimes it helps to unburden oneself in front of a sympathetic audience, the which, I assure you, we are." The Parson nodded in assent, thinking that perhaps Rose had just given him an inroad into this population of troubled souls. "But if you would prefer to remain silent about your trials and tribulations, please, keep mum. Neither I nor the Parson would want to importune you."

"My, I am so unused to such kindness and such gentle speech. Very well then. My story. We had quite a nice little life. I had a husband, Jack, who was an artillery man and we had a child, a little girl name of Matilda. We had a little place in Hackney. As a soldier, he was gone much of the time, but we managed," the story seemed to spill out from Elsie, as if she had been waiting for just such an opportunity, "Well, the last time he came back, he was changed. He said something about a shell exploding nearby and he was unconscious for several days. They took him for dead but he recovered and came home. He had headaches something awful and would wake every night screaming blue murder. Finally he took to drinking. It was the only way he could sleep see? But then he couldn't hold down any job. We was so hard up. Well one day he disappears and he doesn't come back like he usually did. So two days go by and I'm fretting again something terrible, so I picks up Matilda and we go to look for him, down Gin Lanes all over the east end. Finally I find him curled up half insensible in a doorway. I roused him but he was like madman, lunging at me calling me all sorts of names. It broke my heart." At this Elsie teared up, half from the remembrance of her husband's cruel words and in part in anticipation, for the worst was yet to come. "He called me all sorts of names and started beating me. A Bow Street Runner comes by and arrests me for a…a prostitute. I lose my moorings and they tell me I bit the runner's ear off. I am charged and found guilty. They said it was my supposed whoring that drove Jack to drink. They take away my Matilda to grow up in a workhouse. I am put on a hulk and then transported to this place where I am taken as nothing more than a whore. They have made me into what they wrongly accused me of being."

"Well, not anymore," interjected Prendergast. "I am bound and determined to keep you on here."

"Thank you sir and no disrespect, but things are terrible here. You cannot rely on anything lasting. People die all the time."

Both Rose and Prendergast raised their eyebrows as they attempted to absorb what they had just heard, what Elsie walked around carrying inside of herself all the time.

"We will do our best," said the parson quietly, returning to his meal.

"My story is also one of miscarried justice," offered Rose, as if to even up the disclosures. "My betrothed, Garrad was wrongly accused and sent here. I am here to find him."

"Goodness, how brave. Would that I could be reunited with my man and my Matilda…" and at this she broke down into sobbing. Finally with comforting touches from Rose, she recovered some of her composure and offered, "I wish you the best miss."

"Thank you. I fear it will have taken every ounce of his strength to have survived such an ordeal as this place offers."

They ate again for a while in silence. Eventually, the parson, in full awareness of the magnitude of his task and with a small sense of irony, offered, "And I am here to offer whatever spiritual comfort as may seem fitting. Very good stew, by the way. Thank you, Elsie."

IV

All three slept fitfully that night, each preoccupied with their own concerns: the parson, feeling overwhelmed at the prospect of reaching these wounded souls; Rose, daunted by the prospect of venturing further in her quest for Garrad and Elsie; adapting to her new more salubrious placement, but at the same time anxious lest it, like almost everything else good in her life, be taken away.

They were all up early. Eggs were coming to a boil on the stove when Rose heard Elsie hail someone from the front of the cabin where she was beating a rug.

"Gigby! Oh miss! It's Gigby. He's a good old chap. Please, may I talk with him awhile? He has been so good to me," pleaded Elsie.

"Of course, if he is your friend. Sit here on the bench," said Rose indicating the bench set beside the front doorway.

"Well, I say, 'talk', miss, but I do not know his language, but we do our best with signs," said Elsie with a self-conscious laugh.

The parson, hearing the conversation had stepped into the doorway and he with Rose, gazed with some amazement at the tall, dark, lean and graceful aborigine as he approached them, nodding in recognition. They were even more surprised when Elsie and Gigby fell into an animated conversation involving gesticulations of all kinds, sometimes accompanied by grunts of correction or of encouragement.

Rose heard the sound of the eggs bumping into the pot as they boiled and went inside to take them off the stove. Elsie and Gigby continued their conversation. The parson returned to his scriptures and thought.

Rose thought she would try out the piano. She rubbed it with a rag from the kitchen adjusted the seat and played some scales to see if it was in working order. The damp had altered the timbre and a few notes were off but it was quite serviceable. She wondered what she would play. Welling up with emotion, she realized it would have to be the last song she had played for Garrad, "Lowlands Away." She started to tear up at the emotions that tore through her but she persevered, thinking it would be good for her to have some sort of catharsis. The melody came at first very slowly, haltingly but after a few choruses it picked up speed and Rose started to feel her fingers remember the keys and she inserted some of her favorite flourishes.

She continued playing for several minutes until she felt she had exhausted all of her feelings through the song and then sat still, breathing slowly and deeply. She suddenly became aware that Elsie, Gigby and the parson were all gathered behind her with stricken looks on their faces.

"I'm sorry. I must have got carried away. I didn't mean to put on a performance so early in the morning. It's just…"

"No miss," interrupted Elsie. "It's Gigby. If I understand him rightly he says he helped a man and his friend across the mountains some time ago and one of the men kept on singing that song. He sang it so much that Gigby even learned it."

"Lowlands!" intoned Gigby.

Stunned, Rose took several moments to fully digest the possible meaning of this. She weighed the chances. It had to be Garrad.

"Elsie, can you ask our friend Gigby if he could take me to where these men are?" inquired Rose.

"I can try," said Elsie, immediately falling into a sequence of gestures and pronounced facial expressions that they exchanged with each other for several minutes. At times one or the other would look by turns confused and frustrated and their conversation would come to a standstill. At these points, Rose's heart sank. Finally each nodded as if something had been settled.

Finally Elsie translated. "He says he can take you. It is a long and difficult journey with lots of hills. It will take many days and you will have to leave in secret so the guards don't see you and follow."

"And we are far enough from the settlement that no-one would notice you were gone for some time," added Prendergast.

The weight of a decision hung in the group for a few moments. Rose nodded and said, "Yes. Thank you. Elsie, please tell Gigby thank you a million times. I would like to leave as soon as is convenient for Mr. Gigby."

Again, Elsie managed to convey this message to Gigby who then nodded in assent.

V

Two days later Rose felt deeply fortified by the generous servings of mutton stew, porridges and various broths that Elsie managed to conjure up from the environs. Parson

Prendergast had inspected what was to be his little chapel and was busying himself with preparing sermons and whatever other services he might offer to the crushed spirits of this blighted, yet, paradoxically, in its natural abundance, so vibrant and fulsome place.

Elsie seemed to exult in her role of helper. She seemed to adore the parson and was very attentive to Rose's every wish. Showing extreme concern for Rose's well-being on her upcoming trek she fashioned, after gaining Rose's permission, a pair of pantaloons from one of her sturdier dresses from Bahia and stitched together a pair of canvas buskins to wrap around her calves. Somehow Elsie procured a stout pair of boots. Neither Rose nor the parson wished to know from where they came. They were slightly too large for Rose but could be made to fit if lined with some well-placed cloth rags.

The weather cleared and the sky was crystalline blue with a few magnificent towering clouds trimmed with pink as evening fell. All was quiet when Gigby emerged noiselessly from the surrounding trees and nodded, indicating that the time had come for their long journey. He had accomplished what he needed in the settlement and was to return to his people over the mountains. Rose repaired to her room, breathing deeply and slowly in order to subdue her trembling, saying to herself, "This is the last step in my journey," as she looked at the now-faded and worn wish-bracelet she had got in Bahia. It could surely only be days until it finally gave way and her dream became reality. She started to put on her travelling clothes, the britches Elsie had fashioned for her, her bodice and loose coat made from a blanket. When she wrapped her feet in the rags and sank her feet into the boots she smiled, thinking of Gigby's bare calloused feet, how careful she must be and yet how seemingly careless was Gigby of the stones and thorns that lined their path. Finally, she tied the buskins around her calves. Somehow all the clothing and protective gear emboldened her. She stepped out of the cabin. By now the twilight had thickened so that the interstices of the forest were impenetrably black, into which one might safely disappear. All took a deep breath and Rose and Elsie hugged.

"You are so brave Miss," said Elsie.

"We shall see," replied Rose.

"Words cannot express my admiration and gratitude," said the parson, shaking Rose's hand.

"I simply have no choice," replied Rose.

"I understand Miss; you must go where your heart leads you. God bless," said Elsie.

"Godspeed. Until we meet again," said Prendergast gazing intensely into Rose's welling eyes.

Rose and Gigby turned and took a few steps down the track. Rose turned and waved and then, as if by some magical illusion, they disappeared.

VI

Rose followed Gigby closely throughout the night, staying close to him. Fortunately she felt strengthened by Elsie's cooking, for Gigby kept up a good pace. Rose slipped and fell several times and bumped her head frequently on low-hanging branches. She was glad to have the canvas buskins and solid boots for the terrain was rough and it was black as pitch. Despite the hard going she was buoyed up by the strong sentiment that this might be the last leg of her journey. Every now and then she found herself touching the ribbon on her wrist, sensing that at any moment it might give way while knowing that she had days of arduous travel ahead of her.

Just as the fatigue was starting to overcome her and she was feeling dizzy and disoriented, Gigby, pointing at the grey streaks that could be seen in the sky between the overarching trees, indicated that she should sit. He immediately disappeared, returning minutes later bearing the fruits, leaves and berries that were to be their breakfast. She understood that there must be no fire for although they had traveled miles through the night, there was still the chance that smoke would attract unwelcome attention. Rose had brought some food in a sack that Elsie had given her, but decided to try Gigby's food. She found it to be a good decision, for it seemed laden with nutriment that was instantly absorbed by her body, seeming to dissolve her fatigue and growing irritability. They tarried awhile and Rose was able to doze off. When she awoke, sun was sparkling through the treetops and Gigby was standing, ready to go. He gestured for her to follow and they melted into the undergrowth. It seemed clear to Rose that Gigby was following a path, even one that was well-worn to him, for he hesitated not one whit. Rose, try as she might, could not make out what signs he might be following as they climbed and descended a seemingly endless sequence of hills, slopes, gullies and waded across many small streams.

And so they trekked on, day after day, finally reaching the peaks which had the steep, cream-colored scarps of the deepest sections of the mountain range. Rose was spellbound by their majesty and mesmerizing beauty, especially as they captured the rose and honey-tinted lights of dawn and evening. After yet more days of threading their way through the cliffs, scarps and screes of the high mountain range Rose felt that they had started to descend. Such streams as they encountered were heading in the same direction as their footsteps. After several days of descent, they came out upon a bluff.

"Katoomba," Gigby said, one of his very few utterances during the entire trip, and he indicated with a sweep of his arm the dreamlike vista of low rolling hills, of tans, ochres and countless shades of green, dotted with waving copses of shimmering trees that lay in front of them. They paused awhile to take in the swelling majestic grandeur of the scene and presently briskly started their descent on to the rolling plains below. Rose started to feel that this surely must be it. Garrad must be here and she scanned, at every opportunity the vista spread out before her of a sign that might betray his presence, occasionally feeling her bracelet to see if it was still there.

Chapter 9

I

Toby Pegg took a deep swig of his rum bottle as he hunkered down for the night in his drifter, moored on a jetty just off the main channel. He glanced one more time across the rippled jet waters towards Saint Osyth, just to be sure, for it was a moonless night, precisely the kind of night the French visitors and their treasonous cohorts preferred.

There it was. Three long flashes as Jim Varley covered and uncovered his oil lamp some two miles away, at the place where the channel opened up into the North Sea. Toby peered again, rubbing his eyes to be sure and then made off down the slippery jetty as fast as his sea legs would carry him and on down the path towards the Peldon Rose, where he roused Blakesley and Flaxman. They were ready, as if anticipating the visit from Toby and in less than a minute they were assembled outside the pub.

"I suggest Flaxman and I proceed quickly on foot to the jetty on Beggars Creek and conceal ourselves in the bushes. Mr. Pegg, perhaps you could discreetly float there and conceal yourself should we need help."

"Yes sir, just as we arranged. And on my way, I will get Dan Pritchett, for he has a bone or two to pick," replied Toby.

"Good. You have your pistol?" Blakesley inquired of Flaxman.

"Yes, right here," replied Ben, patting his side-pocket.

"Then let us be off."

Ten minutes later, Blakesley and Ben Flaxman were hidden in the bushes to one side of the Beggars Creek jetty. Ten minutes after that they heard a swoosh and saw the shadow as Toby and Dan slid by and concealed themselves behind the mud-bank. Their wait was long, for it would take the interloper an hour or so to sail and scull from Saint Osyth to Beggar's Creek, longer still if one was not thoroughly familiar with the waters, tides and currents.

Ben started to believe that they had made a mistake for it seemed to him that the sky was lightening in the east, perhaps turning a shade of grey as dawn was approaching. By then no-one in their right sense would come. Just as he thought this he heard a noise along the sea wall pathway, a footfall, followed perhaps by an admonishing whisper. Ben and Blakesley made eye contact, each recognizing, with a tightening in their chest, that the moment of confrontation was arriving. The steps got closer. It was two men speaking in very tense lowered tones. They sounded angry. No sooner had this happened than there was a riffling on the water, the creak of a timber and the dull thud of a boat hitting the jetty.

"Je suis ici!" came a hissing voice from the jetty.

"Bien, nous arrivons!" replied one of the two on the sea wall.

This was followed by some mumbled cursing as the man secured his boat to the jetty. Finally, this done, he joined the other two on the sea wall where they started to converse. As Ben Flaxman adjusted his position, he saw one of the men hand what seemed to be a sheaf of notes to the visitor who then handed them a brick shaped brown parcel.

No sooner had this occurred than Blakesley nudged Flaxman indicating that the time had come. They stood up and swiftly stepped out from behind the bushes onto the sea wall. Blakesley raised his pistol at them and yelled out, "Halt your business, in the name of the King!"

As one body the three men, stunned into silence turned to see the silhouettes of Blakesley and Flaxman, both with pistols raised at them.

The Frenchman was the first to recover, "I must warn you gentilhommes, I too have a pistolet and I am very swift and accurate. One of you will die," he said calmly raising his weapon. Up on the sea wall and by the first grey gleaming light of dawn, Flaxman made out the two accomplices, Sir Sydney and Squire Paxton who, unused to such situations, took a step back and froze into immobility.

"I know who you are," said Blakesley, firmly and addressing the Frenchman. "You are Le Renard, French spy. I will know of your dealings with these two men."

"Ah, je regrette, monsieur," replied Le Renard, "that cannot be, c'est un secret."

Paxton finally found some words. "Look, old chap…"

"Sir, I am an adjutant of Rear Admiral Farnborough, not an 'old chap'," stiffly and tersely interrupted Blakesley.

"Of course, my apologies," continued Paxton. "Look, we have cash here…"

"No, you fool," interrupted Sir Sydney.

"...and your share would be considerable."

"Sir, you underestimate my allegiance," responded Blakesley angrily but before he could complete his thought, Dan Pritchett lunged out of the bush and threw himself at Le Renard, sweeping him off the sea wall so that they both tumbled down into the muddy tide-pool below. There, Le Renard seemed more discomfited by the slop that now liberally besmirched his finery such that Dan was able to thump him twice with his ample fists and restrain him by twisting the Frenchman's arm mercilessly. The pistol plopped into the black waters of the estuary.

Blakesley and Flaxman saw the opportunity Pritchett had offered and took it. They bounded towards Sir Sydney and Paxton who, taken utterly by surprise, put up no fight. Blakesley swiftly placed handcuffs on Sir Sydney and then placed them on Paxton who was all the time being restrained by Flaxman.

"Mr. Pegg, are you there?" he called out.

"I am sir," he replied.

"Would you be so kind as to speed ahead and notify constable Pike that we have apprehended three spies? Mr. Pritchett, if you drag our French friend up here I have a spare pair of cuffs for him."

"It would be my pleasure sir."

II

Adjutant Blakesley, Ben Flaxman and Pritchett escorted the three hangdog miscreants to Peldon where they were met by Constable Pike, who was flustered by the enormity of the crime he confronted, it being of far greater import than the usual poaching, trespassing, smuggling and theft with which he was usually concerned. They held the men until dawn when they took the morning stage to Maldon and from there on Chelmsford. There, at the county seat they were charged and sent on to Newgate prison to await trial. They had hoped they would be able to pay for their stay in the prison's "State Section" which was more salubrious and suited for gentlemen of their rank but, to their dismay, their coffers were all but empty and they had to reside with the "common folk". There they spent the rest of their days, questioned frequently as to their knowledge and their contacts. Many called for their execution but it was held by those in power that they were of more value alive than dead, either as sources of information or, as in the case of Le Renard, as a bargaining chip should Britain need to trade a prisoner at some point in the ever-intensifying conflict with the French.

Chapter 10

I

Finally, after two days of descending from the high mountains, Gigby and Rose came upon the rolling verdant hills she had beheld from the outlook bluff. She was as amazed at the lush meadows that seemed to stretch in every direction as she was pleased by the relative ease of walking.

It was at this point that Gigby held his hand up as if to pause, as if he had heard something. He beckoned for Rose to sit while he climbed up a grassy slope atop a curved hillock. There he stood and surveying each of the cardinal points, sang out in what seemed to be worship of the land, the sky, the streams, the animals, the birds, the plants—all of surrounding nature. Rose could not make out the precise meaning of what Gigby was singing, but it was so poignant, so beautiful that iy seemed to vibrate deep into her heart. She felt deeply thankful to Gigby for this song, or series of songs, for it captured not only her deep sense of gratitude at having reached this more hospitable terrain, but also a profound mysterious sense of gratitude to the earth itself and the sustenance it gave.

Finally Gigby finished. He sat in silent contemplation for a while and then, with the air of someone who has accomplished a necessary task, descended the hillock and indicated that it was now time to proceed.

As they came over one of the hillocks and cleared the copse of dusky green trees, they beheld a mound of stones with a cross on top. Rose's heart seemed to leap into her throat and instinctively she felt for her bracelet. It was gone, broken off, finally worn away. She gasped in painful recognition of the fact that this pile of stones was her reunion. Garrad lay beneath these rocks. She started to weep uncontrollably all the tears that had been gathering as a storm deep inside her all these past months upon months of travel. She fell to her knees, crying, "No! No!"

She felt a warm touch on her shoulder that calmed her. It was Gigby's hand. After several minutes of weeping, she regained some small amount of composure and turned to look at Gigby. She felt lost. What could she possibly do now?

Gigby simply shook his head and nodded in the direction they were to go. Rose struggled to her feet, wobbling, since the surge of emotion had taken away her sense of her own body and followed Gigby, haltingly, wondering to herself where on earth they might be heading and feeling conflicted because she knew her place to be by Garrad's grave. Gigby turned every few yards and encouraged her in her forward movement.

They descended into a gully which had a stream in it and followed the stream for several hundred yards. Eventually the gully widened out into a broad flat valley and the stream joined a river, some thirty feet wide. Rose was feeling deep fatigue and growing annoyance at being diverted from her mourning of Garrad and was just about to protest when Gigby stopped and pointed downstream. There, in the distance was a human form, lifting boulders in mid-stream, knee deep in the fast-flowing river, bronzed deeply by the sun, glistening in the spray that sparkled in the sun all around him.

Rose quickened her pace. Gigby let her overtake as if he knew the couple would want to be alone. Rose called out Garrad's name but at first he did not hear over the sound of the water rushing all around him. Suddenly, as if feeling her presence, he looked up and around, finally seeing her stumbling hurriedly down the grassy bank. Stunned, and at first not believing his eyes were seeing that which he had longed to behold for so long, through such agonies, he stood stock still, only able to address the reality of this being Rose running down the river bank when she was able to breathlessly call out, "Garrad, it's me!" as she broke down into gasping tears and started to wade into the river across the stones of the fish-trap. Garrad snapped back into his senses and pushed against the waters towards her. Finally, waist deep in the middle of the river, they met, touched each other's faces as if to reassure themselves of the reality of each other and they embraced melting into one.

"But how?" was all Garrad could utter.

"I told you. Just whistle and I'll come running," her eyes sparkling with that old indomitable humour.

Chapter 11

A stiff westerly wind whipped the grey waves of the English Channel into a froth as Ben Flaxman stepped out of the warm shelter and onto the windswept wharf at Portsmouth. He pulled his hat down firmly onto his head and tightened his cloak around his shoulders. The quayside was bustling with activity as the stout three-masted, square-rigged ship heaved at the dockside, seeming to wrestle impatiently at its stays as if eager to depart.

Ben gazed around at the scene; soldiers, adventurers and hopefuls lining up around the gangplank to get on board; longshoremen heaving the last provisions and supplies on board; horses, cages of fowl, bales of hay and sacks of vegetables and provender swinging overhead; peddlers attempting to sell their wares until the last possible moment; those left behind crying or gazing with grim, empty eyes.

There was no-one to bid farewell to Ben. He faced a journey of more than one hundred days to the other side of the earth. There would be plague, scurvy, rough seas, the bloody flux and loneliness. But go he must. He had betrayed his daughter once. He must not do so again.

Printed in the United States
By Bookmasters